THE   LOST   WORLD   OF   EVEREST

THE LOST WORLD
OF
EVEREST

by

BERKELEY GRAY

THE CHILDREN'S PRESS
LONDON AND GLASGOW

P Pipe.

PRINTED IN GREAT BRITAIN

CONTENTS

To

K. GLEN

who read this story in manuscript and whose
generous enthusiasm for it leads me to hope that
it will go down all right with all you other chaps.

B. G.

Chapter One

THE TOP OF THE WORLD

" Big Bill " Gresham paused as the icy wind, carrying needle-points of frozen snow, rose to the force of a blizzard and threatened to tear him from his precarious hold.

He glanced down and saw Reggie and Peter resting, too. They were clinging to the treacherous ice-face, grotesque-looking creatures in their cold-resisting suits and oxygen helmets, only vaguely visible in the blinding snow smother.

Young Lord Gresham grinned within his own headgear; he forgot the gruelling hardships and the stark perils of their present position, and he grinned.

The last lap . . .

Everest nearly conquered . .

Bill Gresham glowed with the glorious thrill of it. Already they were on top of the world; only another two or three thousand feet to go, and . . . Only! A short enough distance in actual measurement, as compared with the miles they had climbed. But this final lap was the supreme test, where every foot gained had to be battled for with grim tenacity and dogged determination.

Bill signalled. Once again he struggled onwards and upwards, laboriously cutting the steps in the steeply-ascending slope of glassy ice. His mood was one of confident triumph; to-day, he felt, all the trying weeks of painstaking preparation were to be rewarded. He had felt certain of success ever since they had started out at daybreak from the last camp.

Camp No. 6—27,500 feet up!

And now they had conquered another thousand feet . . . This time they'd do it! Old Everest was growling and snarling, but to-day she was going to be whacked—at last!

Physically perfect, specially trained, the three intrepid young climbers were thoroughly acclimatised to the ferocious conditions with which they had to contend. Their rubber cold-resisting suits —so light that their movements were not hampered—and their oxygen gear would have been of little use without their own skill and determination and great powers of endurance.

Roped together, they were fighting desperately for every inch they gained. The blizzard shrieked madly about them as though furious that these puny humans should have invaded its lofty fastness. So rarefied was the atmosphere that it contained only one-third of the normal amount of oxygen in each pint of air breathed. At such heights human and animal life cannot be maintained for long; the heart and the other organs begin to lose their powers . . .

But the daring young climbers were not affected, for they breathed life-giving oxygen which permitted them to retain their normal faculties and strength. Grimly, fiercely, they pressed on. They no longer thought of the long and weary marches, extending over many weeks, which had brought them to the base of the mighty Himalayas and Everest the Giant. All that was over— just as the long climb from camp to camp up the cruel slopes of Everest was over.

Glancing down, Big Bill saw that Reggie Pickles was pointing into the smother . . . And Bill turned his head. He grinned appreciatively. A mile away, and perhaps a thousand feet higher, soared a little white monoplane . . . Bobby Simson doing his stuff . . . Good old Bobby! Keeping his eye on the climbers and reporting their progress by radio to the Base Camp . . . How far away and vaguely distant the Base Camp seemed now! Yet, measured in actual miles, it was only just round the corner, so to speak.

Bill waved a cheery hand. It was doubtful if the man in the plane saw the movement. The snow-smother and the mist blurred everything, and the sturdy little machine was battling grimly against the treacherous winds and cross-currents. A sudden flurry of snowflakes and it vanished altogether.

All the same, Bill Gresham was cheered and comforted. It was nice to know that friends were so near . . . And yet so far! Bobby Simson and his plane had vanished like a mirage, as though they had no real existence.

The last lap!

It seemed to Big Bill, as the blizzard swirled and hooted about him, that an absolute whirlwind raged at the top of the ridge—the ridge which was their first objective of the day. Once they gained that spot, Bill believed, they would have to make a detour and then climb another great couloir before they could reach the absolute summit . . . before they could claim ultimate victory.

The ridge-top and the sky were obscured by restless clouds of tossing, whirling vapour. There was something awe-inspiring, something peculiarly *vindictive,* in the ceaseless movements of the mist. Even Reggie Pickles and Peter Fraser, lower down the ice-face, sensed the mystery and positive *threat* of something unknown yet tremendous.

A whirling eddy of the mist, as cold as the touch of Death's hand, came down the icy slope and enveloped Big Bill; and in spite of his special clothing he was chilled and half-paralysed with the incredible cold.

" Trying to scare us, eh?" he grunted. " Nothing doing, old friend! You can bluster as much as you like, but we are used to your tantrums by this time!"

As though in answer, as though Everest herself had heard the challenge and was angry, the whole air became filled with a deafening drumming roar. There was an unearthly, terrifying note in that sound, and as it penetrated into the interior of Big Bill's helmet he half turned and stared upwards. At the same moment Reggie Pickles flung out a hand, pointing.

" Look!" came a muffled cry.

But Bill had seen. Illusory, yet startlingly real, grotesque and gigantic shadows swayed and writhed on the mist clouds; they were like living figures from some nightmare world, neither human nor animal.

Were they the shadows of the three climbers, reflected and distorted by some freak of the atmosphere, or were they . . . ?

Before Bill could find an answer to the question the spectral figures were surrounded and enveloped by a shroud of mist and vanished. And the strident roar of the blizzard arose to a wild and fiendish shriek. That icy clutch tore grimly at the young climbers, seeking to dislodge them and send them hurtling down the ice-face they had so laboriously climbed.

Bill Gresham clenched his teeth as the force of the squall eased. The sooner they were over this ridge the better!

As the icy blast pulled at him with the power of an almost living, malignant intelligence, he struggled on, fighting with all his brawn and muscle to gain the ridge's summit.

Strong and fit as he was, he was nearly spent by the time he succeeded. The mist swirling above his head cleared for a moment and permitted him to gaze down a long icy slope, even steeper than the one they had just climbed.

It was an unpleasant shock. Bill had expected to find level ground up here and bare rock over which they could progress with comparative ease.

The others joined him. They crouched there on hands and knees, their axes sunken into the ice in order to prevent their being swept away by the merciless hurricane. Reggie and Peter needed no telling of the peril of their position. Something was wrong. According to their maps, they should have reached a rocky plateau . . . For weeks the upper slopes of Everest had been surveyed and mapped by the expedition's planes. . . .

Bill, trying to penetrate the blinding smother of

mist and snow, felt a sudden sense of relief. The awful confusion of the atmosphere had in no way changed, and the terrifying roar was greater than ever; but for a moment the mist had cleared again and he had seen, away to the left, a path of ice. . . . It was no more than a yard wide, which seemed to lead to a frowning face of rock where they might obtain protection. He pointed . . . and stood up.

It seemed that the elements had been awaiting this move, for no sooner was Lord Bill on his feet than a current of air like something tangible and solid struck him with the force of a physical blow.

It came slantingly from above, felling him with the brutality of a bludgeon stroke. He slithered over the edge of the ridge, the safety rope twanging, and a moment later all three climbers were shooting down the mist-hidden icy slope, gathering speed with the awful terror of a Hurricane Fighter in a power dive.

There was nothing they could do to check that horrific descent into the unknown; their very brains were numbed by the swiftness of the catastrophe. Even in this dread moment, however, Bill was conscious of one bewildering fact.

There was no rush of air past their hurtling bodies! The terrific wind was carrying them with it, and the wind was screaming down the ice slope.

It was as though they had been caught in the suction of a giant vacuum cleaner.

Down . . . down! Faster and faster!

The surface of the glacier was like polished glass, hard and smooth and as steep as the roof of a house. Bunched together now, Big Bill and his companions shot down with appalling swiftness, for, in addition to the natural momentum of their descent, they were forced by the down current.

They were capable of one thought only . . . the thought of imminent death. A collision with any hummock or ridge would not merely kill them; it would disintegrate them as surely as though they had been hit by an exploding shell.

Then, gradually at first, but with rapidly-increasing effect, a brake was applied. The surface of the slope was softening! Almost before they realised it, they were plunging through powdery snow. Their rapidly-descending bodies caused the snow to shoot up in a white spray. It became deeper and softer, and they ploughed into it, drove into it, until incredible masses gathered round them and above them.

At last their mad descent was at an end—and they were buried!

Their very brains dulled, they lay for some time inert, scarcely believing that they still lived. They all had a vague feeling that they had left their stomachs somewhere on the upper slopes. . . Big Bill Gresham, the biggest and strongest of the three, was first to make a move.

Walls of soft snow pressed upon him, and he groped about with his hands in the darkness of that strange prison. He felt a leg which was not his own, and the leg moved. He thrust it aside and tore at the snow walls, burrowing grimly but without panic. Bill Gresham had never in his life been known to lose his head, and he did not lose it now. Yet if he had given way to panic none could have blamed him.

He fought the snow calmly, determinedly. He knew that Reggie and Peter were crawling in his wake, although they were still too dazed and dumbfounded for conversation. To his infinite satisfaction, the snow yielded easily; and foot by foot, yard by yard, he dug his way out of the icy prison.

Suddenly an immense mass of the snow cracked and crumbled, and daylight struck Bill blindingly. Something else struck him, too . . . something which his senses, his reason, refused to credit.

A wave of warm, tranquil air!

He felt it in spite of his cold-resisting suit and his oxygen helmet. He stumbled waist-high into the open, with Reggie and Peter just behind. None had received injuries, and they were still too bewildered to fully realise the amazing significance of the changed conditions. Their brains, as yet, could only tell them that they were on the uppermost slopes of Mount Everest, that they had met with a major disaster, and that they were hopelessly lost.

Big Bill took off his headgear and drew in a deep breath of warm, grateful air.

"Well, boys, Everest wins—again!" he said sadly.

Then he started. He jumped. A wild shout escaped him.

For in that split second he knew that something was insanely wrong.

The air was warm and liberally charged with oxygen. . . . And it should have been lots of degrees below zero and so rarefied as to be scarcely breathable! He blinked and shook himself and stared . . . . and stared.

"Impossible!" he muttered thickly.

He looked at the others, his eyes round. They had shed their oxygen gear, too, and they were staring in the same incredulous way.

"Impossible," muttered Reggie, "is right!"

They all saw something which simply could not be . . . . something at which their minds boggled. They *were* on the uppermost slopes of

Everest; they had slithered down a couple of thousand feet, perhaps, but they were still on top of the world, over 27,000 feet up, in a region that should have been nothing but icy wastes and fierce blizzards and treacherous glaciers.

Yet the scene before them, spread out like a magic panorama, was fantastic in its utter impossibility; and at the same time crystal clear in its positive reality. A crazy contradiction.

They were on the higher slope of a great basin or valley, with rolling masses of unbroken virgin snow all about them. Above, the white slopes were lost in misty vapour which eddied and swirled with a curiously rotary motion. Now and again wisps of the mist, ragged and torn, raced down the valley's side until they lost themselves in the clearer atmosphere. Up there, the powerful " down " wind was like something alive.

But the three adventurous climbers of the Everest Expedition gave only one glance at the upper slopes; they were dumb with amazement by the scene which was spread before their eyes lower down.

Their mad descent had halted them about half-way down the great basin. Below and in front of them, stretching for several miles, lay the lower slopes and the valley's floor. The snow grew thinner and thinner until it finally gave way to rocky ground of a deep reddish colour, curiously streaked with brilliant orange and scarlet.

Lower still, vegetation began to appear; coarse grasses in sprawling patches until, at last, on the floor itself, the vegetation became dense. Woods! Miniature forests! Thickly growing trees and wide stretches of rough meadowland, interspersed with turbulent streams.

A world hitherto unknown . . . . the first glimpse of the Lost World of Everest!

Chapter Two

MYSTERY VALLEY

Lord William Everard Cornwallis Gresham was the first to speak and his comment was characteristic.

" Turned out nice again!" he said coolly.

Reggie Pickles, his fair hair standing up like a mop, his fresh young face pink with excitement, attempted to speak but only succeeded in making a queer gurgling noise.

" We'll get out of these togs," continued Big Bill. " They're stuffy, and it's pretty warm here. No reason why we shouldn't have a look round."

Peter Fraser, who, like Reggie, had been having trouble with his larynx, suddenly found his voice. He let out a great bellow, and pointed down the slopes, his hand quivering.

" But look!" he yelled excitedly. " Look down there, Bill!"

" I'm looking."

" Well! Can't you *see*?"

" Of course I can see."

" Then why the dickens don't you seem surprised?" grumbled Peter, rubbing his eyes. " You haven't forgotten by any chance that we're on the top of Everest?"

Big Bill grinned.

" No good getting all hot, old chap," he replied coolly. " This thing is staring us in the face and we've got to accept it—although common sense tells us that it can't be. But it is! So what's the good of getting excited?"

That was Big Bill Gresham all over; always matter-of-fact, always cheerfully calm. Nothing ever flurried his unruffled poise. Some people called him stolid, but they did him an injustice. His father, the Duke of Dunstable, had long since given Bill up as hopeless; and even Bill's elder brother, who was an M.P., and a coming force in politics, had got into the habit of wincing whenever he heard of Bill's latest exploits. The family never knew what he was going to do next. They had heartily approved of the Everest Expedition because it had satisfactorily disposed of Bill for quite a useful number of months.

" Boys," said Bill happily, " we've hit the Biggest Thing of the century, and I don't mean maybe."

He was a quick thinker in any emergency, but he found it unnecessary to call upon his wits now. The dullest intelligence could perceive that this hidden valley on Everest's upper slopes was a natural phenomenon—in all likelihood an extinct volcanic crater. Not so extinct, either, for the warmth of the air seemed capable of only one explanation; heat, natural heat, was rising from the basin's floor.

"Look here, skipper, this thing's fantastic," ejaculated Peter Fraser, at last.

Peter was hard-boiled and solid and his imaginative faculty was not highly developed; a great chap to have with you on a difficult job, and as brave as a lion . . . . but dependent entirely upon the leadership of another.

"Why haven't we seen all this from the air?" he went on, with a comprehensive wave of his hand. "You went up with Bobby on reconnaissance flights time after time—and so did I. So did Reggie. We photographed Everest from every angle, too. Why didn't we see all this?"

Big Bill pointed upwards.

"There's your answer."

"I don't get it," said Peter, staring.

"Remember the storms we struck?" asked Bill significantly. "When we were in the plane, I mean. Even on the sunniest days there were patches of disturbed atmosphere which we couldn't approach."

"Gad, that's right," said Reggie, nodding. "Bobby and I had the same experience. As soon as we got near those storm centres the old bus was tossed about like a cork, and we had to sheer off."

" Exactly," said Bill. " I'm no scientist, Mustard, but it's clear enough that this warm air, continually rising, creates a tremendous and perpetual disturbance of the upper air. Look at it! Now we can understand that awful down current."

The sky was completely hidden by the eternal mist which formed a cloud far above. From the air, as the comrades could verify, that cloud looked trifling and normal . . . . just one of the blizzards which always rage round the peak. But it was sufficient to keep air observers away, and to conceal this amazing valley.

In every direction the scene was the same. The basin formed a perfect cup, with vegetation at the bottom, then rocky slopes, then soft snow, and, finally, a thousand feet or so of sheer glassiness, where the temperature was below zero, merging into the upper mists.

" I say, dash it!" Reggie Pickles—" Mustard " to his friends—was on his feet, and he was looking blank. " How the dickens are we going to get out of this?"

" Just what I was thinking," said Peter.

" We lost our axes when we started slithering down," continued Reggie breathlessly. " Good gad! The thing's impossible ! We'll never make the climb!''

Big Bill nodded.

'' I figured that out five minutes ago,'' he said. '' After a struggle we might manage to fight our way through this soft snow, but without an axe between us we'd never climb the ice field. Over a thousand feet of sheer glass as steep as a church spire.''

'' Then what are we going to do?'' asked Peter.

'' Easy,'' said Lord Gresham coolly. '' As we can't climb up, we'll descend.''

'' That's an idea,'' exclaimed Reggie, his eyes shining. '' Might as well do some exploring, eh? Ye gods and little fishes! Look at those cataracts! Look at the way they converge out of the melting snow and form into huge torrents. And what becomes of the torrents? Worth looking into, what?''

'' So let's look into it,'' said Bill lightly.

His tranquil state of mind was something at which to marvel. Reggie and Peter, unlike their leader, could not yet adjust themselves to the changed conditions. Peter Fraser was only now aware of the mighty torrents Reggie had pointed out; and now that he was aware of them, he heard their deep-throated roar.

Indeed, the very atmosphere throbbed with vibratory sound. Vaguely from above came the eternal boom of the storm, whilst from below the tumult of the rushing water made a fitting accompaniment. Where the three young men stood in the snow all was calm and tranquil.

They plunged downwards and soon found that the soft snow was melting everywhere. It was melting all round the basin, and it ran in a thousand trickling streams down the rocky slopes; these streams joined one another and became swift torrents. These had worn deep channels in the rock.

Lower still the torrents again joined forces, until, from all sides, there were perhaps half-a-dozen mighty cataracts hurtling across the basin's floor. In the very centre, where the various streams converged, there was a mountain of spray rising for hundreds of feet into the air.

But what became of the stupendous volume of water, the melted snows of the upper slopes? In some way it vanished into the mountain.

Presently, as the trio reached the end of the snows, they found the hard rocks streaming with water, through which they splashed. And from the lower slopes the air which met them was so moist and warm that they were bathed in perspiration. Big Bill called a halt.

" Better shed these suits," he said.

It was a relief to do so.

" Look at this rock," continued Bill. " As hard as iron and every colour of the rainbow. Volcanic, as sure as a gun. Millions of years ago this was the crater of an active volcano."

" Where do you get that ' millions of years ago,' skipper?" asked Reggie uneasily. " What about this heat? Where's it coming from? If you ask me, this crater is about as extinct as Donald Duck!"

Peter was looking puzzled.

" I can't understand why nobody has ever *seen* this," he said blankly. " Hang it, we're not the first people to climb Everest and planes have flown over it lots of times."

" Dear old Peter, it's simple," explained Lord Bill, smiling. " We're *within* the crater, and to us it looks pretty large."

" Not only looks," said Reggie. " It is pretty large."

" Yes, Mustard, but it's actually only a pin-point on one of the upper glaciers of the mountain," continued Bill. " Just a patch with a blizzard raging round about it. Air observers— ourselves included—have always taken it for an ordinary commonplace blizzard, like all the other blizzards. But no plane has ever flown *into* it. I doubt if any plane could do so without getting cracked up."

" Nothing like being cheerful," said Reggie. " I was thinking, perhaps, that Bobby Simson . . ."

" Better forget Bobby," interrupted Bill. " There's no denying we're in a mess, but it's no good worrying about it. We've made a discovery that will startle the world—always provided that we get back to the world to tell our little story."

" Let's get on," said Peter gruffly. " Might as well see all there is to be seen now we're here. Who would have thought, when we started out this morning . . . Wonder what the others will be thinking when they get no word from us ? Can't you see the newspaper headlines when the news is flashed home? ' Everest Claims Three More Victims '— ' Why Continue This Insane Folly '?"

" Who cares?" said Big Bill, with a laugh.

Rid of their rubber suits and headgear, they descended the rocky ground at a half run, splashing through pools and rivulets. Lower down, however, these streams became well divided, and they were able to avoid them. The vegetation, when they came to it, was a curiously sickly green— owing to the fact, perhaps, that direct sunshine never penetrated the shroud of mist which always curtained the sky.

Conversation became difficult, for the terrific roar of the converging cataracts soon grew deafening. They found themselves on level ground at last. Skirting a swift torrent which tumbled and jostled, they went ploughing through rank weeds and grasses. Then they were beneath the trees. . . .

Strange trees, unlike any they had ever seen, with enormous coarse leaves, and each leaf yellowish-green in colour. The air under this sticky canopy was strangely heavy, and so humid with heat that the explorers unconsciously slowed their movements.

At close quarters everything looked different.

The trees were bigger, and they were not growing closely together, as it had appeared from above. It was possible to walk between the great trunks and to see a fairly wide vista ahead. And everywhere there was an uncanny, awe-inspiring desolation. Those things which should have been present were absent. Not a bird, not a sign of any living creature. Not even a fluttering insect. Whatever life existed in this strange valley, it was vegetable life only. And even this seemed bloated, distorted, and unreal.

As the comrades walked, their feet sank deeply and soggily into a carpet of rotting leaves. The heat was heavy and moist, and in spite of it " Mustard " Pickles shivered.

" Pretty foul, what?" he said, looking uneasily at the others. " There's something ghastly about this place, you fellows. Unnatural, I mean. It even *smells* nasty, dash it!''

They did not hear all his words, for the roaring throb in the air was now terrific. But Bill and Peter, too, had noticed the peculiarly nauseous odour—an emanation, no doubt, from the unhealthy-looking vegetation. But they pressed on, eager to explore further—eager, in spite of their acute discomfort, their growing reluctance and unease.

Emerging from the trees and leaving the wood behind, they found a big open space confronting them; they were getting towards the centre of the basin now, and to right and to left there were other patches of woodland.

Straight ahead, however, lay rocky ground, and within a hundred yards the vast cloud of spray arose where the torrent vanished. In such close proximity as this the thing was awe-inspiring. Deafened, stunned, they stood and watched. Big Bill was the first to make a move forward.

Advancing, he reached the rocky edge of a great gash in the valley's floor—an irregular hole, many hundreds of feet across, into which poured, from every side, a number of great cataracts. From the centre the spray arose. Bill stood there fascinated, and the others joined him. It was staggering to realise that all those millions of tons of water were disappearing into the heart of Everest.

Reggie Pickles moved even nearer to the lip of the abyss and gazed down with fascinated eyes. He shouted something, but the others did not hear him; they could only see the movement of his lips. At their feet was a sheer drop, but it was impossible to tell what lay below. The water swirled and tossed in a frenzy of foam, circling in a terrifying whirlpool, with the spray rising in dense clouds.

Suddenly Bill Gresham stiffened.

Into his eyes came a look of incredulous wonder. His glance had strayed to the right of the spot where they stood, and the rocky face of the giant hole was no longer smooth; instead of a continuation of the smooth surface, great steps appeared in the rock, and they vanished beneath one of the roaring cataracts. As the water hurtled over the edge there was a space left . . . and the steps went down and down, hugging the rock face, until they vanished into the vague cloud of spray.

And those steps were not natural formations— they were *hewn*—and only Man could have hewn them!

Chapter Three

THE THINGS IN THE TUNNEL

It was something of a phenomenon for Lord William Gresham to reveal any sign of excitement; but he was so excited now that he nearly toppled over the edge of the abyss in his eagerness to see more.

"Great Scott! Look at that!" he yelled, gesticulating. "Steps! Steps leading down into the unknown depths."

"Take it easy, Bill . . ." began Peter.

"Take it easy, my foot!" roared Bill. "Can't you see? They're man-made steps, you chump! We thought we were the first human beings to set foot in this valley—but we're not!"

His companions looked at him helplessly. They had only heard his words vaguely, and even now they could not understand his unusual agitation. Even when they followed the direction of his pointing finger they still failed to understand.

But they comprehended clearly enough when he moved along the edge of the great pit and made as if to lower himself over the rock. Reggie clutched at him and drew him back.

"What's the idea?" he shouted. "Suicide?"

"Steps!" bawled Bill, with his mouth close to Mustard's ear. "Leading downwards. Explore."

He pulled himself free, and recklessly lowered his lithe body over the edge. There was a treacherous pathway of rock no more than three feet wide a man's height below. Reggie gulped in horror as he saw his leader carelessly drop.

One slip and he would plunge. . . . But Big Bill was not the kind of fellow to slip, and even if he had been capable of hearing the warnings of his companions he would have taken no notice. He always knew what he wanted and nobody could ever stop him.

After a brief moment of hesitation, Reggie and Peter followed. Greatly as they disliked the enterprise, they had no intention of allowing Bill Gresham out of their sight.

Thus, within a minute or two, they were cautiously descending the rough-hewn, slippery, treacherous steps. On one side of them was the rock face and on the other the glassy inner surface of the falling water. It was a weird and awe-inspiring experience.

Soon they were surrounded by a misty mysterious gloom, but there was not sufficient light for them to see their way distinctly. After they had descended some distance they were aware of a curious change. The deafening roar of the water, instead of increasing, as one would have supposed, grew perceptibly less; and lower still it dwindled to a mere subdued throbbing.

" Something to do with the rock formation, I suppose," shouted Big Bill. " Who cares, anyway? Either of you chaps know anything about the laws of acoustics?"

" Never mind the bally laws of acoustics, ' growled Reggie. " What's the big idea of coming down here, Bill? I suppose you know you're crazy, don't you?"

" Haven't you noticed?"

" Noticed what?"

" The steps, fathead!" grinned Bill. " Great Scott! You're both as blind as bats! Can't you see that they've been carved out of the virgin rock?" He pointed. " Look at them closely. You can see the marks made by the hewers' implements."

Without waiting to hear their comments, he pressed on. Lower and lower! And then the steps ended, and Bill Gresham found himself in a wide cavern. A roofless cavern, through the top of which hurtled the mass of falling water.

There was a great hole in the floor, with a wide rocky space all round—space enough for the three explorers to walk in safety and comfort. They gazed upon the great body of water as it tumbled like something solid into the hole in the floor.

" But what happens to it?" asked Peter dizzily.

It was a sight to make them reel with astonishment. The water, in coming through the upper opening, knitted itself into a smooth-sided body and shot into the floor opening with scarcely any spray, leaving a clearance of some yards all round.

Fascinated, the comrades approached the edge and gazed over. . . . And if they had been awe-stricken before, they were almost terrified now. They felt, rather than saw, that they were staring down into a bottomless void, and their ears were smitten by an indescribable tumult of sound which seemed to come from a great, great distance.

But this was not all. The void beneath them was full of an unearthly glow, as though lit by an interior fire, and the ever-present spray created beautiful and fantastic " rainbows," which flickered and shimmered and danced in ever-changing formations.

" Good gad!" Reggie spoke in a hushed voice. " This water's falling for *miles,* you chaps! I mean, you can't hear it strike the bottom. . . . I mean, dash it! Perhaps there isn't any bottom, what? And where does this strange light come from?"

" Never mind the light," said Peter Fraser,

keeping a grip on himself with difficulty. " Didn't you hear what Bill said a minute ago? Those steps we came down. . . . Man-made steps! But who could have . . ."

" More man-made steps!" interrupted Lord Gresham, pointing. " Come on, boys! This is getting thrilling. I'm getting more kick out of this than I ever got out of climbing Everest!"

" You're telling us!" gurgled Reggie.

They saw for the first time that the sides of the roofless cavern were honeycombed here and there by black gaps which looked like caves or tunnel entrances. Some of them were so small they could not be entered; others were as big as railway tunnels, but beyond reach owing to the fact that they were high up the cavern's side.

One of the latter, however, was provided with a rock-hewn stairway—a stairway so even, so accurately carved, that any lingering doubt which Mustard and Peter might have harboured was dispelled. That stairway had been cut by expert hands—and the hands had been guided by a skilled, intelligent brain.

They ran round the ledge eagerly, and then up the steps. At the top they found the tunnel gleaming with moisture and penetrating mysteriously into the unknown. At the time they did not quite realise why they could see, but they observed that the sides of the tunnel were worn as smooth as glass, and from its depths came a current of warm, dry air. It brought with it a curious tang.

" Smoke!" ejaculated Peter, startled.

" I'm not sure," said Big Bill slowly. " But if it *is* smoke. . . . But what's the good of guessing?"

He led the way. Caution was necessary, for the tunnel sloped steeply downwards and the floor was smooth and wet. Skidding was easy. In places the tunnel twisted, and now and again it took such a sharp downward turn that steps had been cut in order to make the going easier. The edges of the steps were rounded and smooth.

Bill Gresham paused, and bent down.

" Something funny about these steps," he said. " They couldn't have been worn like this by human feet—or animal feet, either. They're not merely worn in the centre, where people would tread; they're worn all over alike."

" How do you mean?" asked Peter, puzzled.

Big Bill did not answer. Even now, so excited were they by the extraordinary events, they did not appreciate the startling fact that the darkness was not absolute, as by all the laws of nature it should have been. In some strange and inexplicable way they could still *see* the tunnel sides and floor. Yet they could not see one another!

They only knew that they did not collide with the walls or stumble over unseen steps. Deeper and deeper they penetrated—until, at long last, the descent eased and now they found the tunnel more or less level. It had taken a turn here, a sharp turn, narrowing at the same time. They rounded the corner and jerked to a standstill.

" Look!" muttered Peter, a catch in his voice.

Ahead, in the strange darkness, they saw a number of reddish spots. . . . Glowing, luminous points, moving stealthily and relentlessly towards them.

" Eyes!" whispered Reggie breathlessly.

" And trouble!" said Big Bill, feeling for the gun he always carried.

But his fingers closed over a small electric torch and he jerked it out. Until that moment he had forgotten that he had it on him. As he was about to press the switch he was aware of a strange sensation, as though he had unwittingly touched some exposed electric wires.

" Hey, what the . . ."

The redly-luminous eyes were coming nearer and nearer, and a dreadful paralysis took Bill Gresham in its grip. He did not know it, but his companions were affected in exactly the same way.

Nearer, nearer came the Eyes. . . .

With a tremendous effort, as his limbs seemed

to be stiffening into stone, Big Bill managed to press the switch of his torch and a beam of white light shot across the tunnel. . . .

And the climbers of Everest saw—men! But such men as they had never dreamed of in their wildest nightmares!

Chapter Four

THE MYSTERIOUS
ANIMAL-MEN

THERE were about six of them, and while four remained in the shadow, two others were caught in the full beam of Lord Gresham's spot-light.

There were squeals, curiously thin and un-human, as the two figures reeled away from the direct light, their hands going up to their faces as though in protection. During that brief moment the three young explorers had a full glimpse of the Tunnel Men.

Scantily dressed in a waist-garment of some coarse matting, they were a pale brownish-yellow in colour; a sickly, repulsive shade, as though the very skin, and the flesh beneath it, was dead. Their features were coarse and cunning and cruel, and suggestive of both Tibetan and Indian blood. Their eyes glowed like red fires. . . . Luminous eyes in the heads of human beings. . . . Eyes which burned like lamps. . . . Eyes which enabled their owners to see in the dark!

As though Nature had not made them suf-ficiently grotesque, their hair, matted and tangled and profuse, was a dead flat white. Such were the strange creatures who lurked in this subterranean tunnel of Everest.

The torchlight beam played steadily, without shifting in the slightest degree. . . . For Big Bill was standing as immovable as a statue. He could shift neither limb nor muscle. That dread paralysis had gripped him more than ever—and his comrades, too. Like him, they were stricken.

Accompanying this utter helplessness they felt a painful tingling and throbbing within their bodies. Yet their senses remained unimpaired, and they were thus condemned to stand helpless, at the mercy of the Tunnel Men.

Bill Gresham's sensations were mixed; but the emotion which gripped him strongest of all was—incredulity. He could see that the creatures about him were unarmed; and, indeed, they struck him as being primitive, untamed savages, for their finger-nails were growing like claws and their faces were full of stupid, animal-like wonder.

One of them came slightly nearer, and venture-somely reached out a hand towards Big Bill. A shock penetrated to every inch of the boy's vitals, and his elbow—which was nearest the reaching hand—burned with excruciating agony. A cry of pain arose in his throat but never found utterance, for his vocal cords were powerless.

The reaching hand was withdrawn, and the agony subsided, leaving an acute sense of " pins and needles." Amazing as it was, impossible as it seemed, the paralysing influence actually emanated from the very bodies of the Tunnel Men! They carried with them an invisible aura of— what?

Electricity? Or was it something different? Something which science had not yet discovered?

It was a problem which intrigued Bill Gresham mightily. He realised that he was helpless, and that these unearthly creatures might be dangerous; but he was able to think clearly and coolly. They were human beings without question—but the product, apparently of some subterranean pit. The possibilities which were thus vouchsafed to Bill almost dazed him.

What was this amazing secret of Everest?

Out of the corner of his eye, for he could not move even his eye muscles, he saw the Tunnel Men creeping about, avoiding the light beam, shading their eyes from its reflecting rays by their hideous claw-like hands. Even the indirect glow of light seemed to hurt their eyes.

One of the creatures gathered courage; he suddenly jumped forward and his paw closed over Peter Fraser's arm. Peter shuddered from head to foot, but no sound left his fixed lips; he tottered and crashed to the rock floor—lying there exactly as he had stood, like a fallen lay-figure, grotesque and pitiful.

Instantly the Tunnel Men advanced nearer, their eyes cruel and wicked. They jabbered amongst themselves, and Big Bill experienced another shock. The language, for the main part, was a mere gibberish, but he had a good knowledge of the local Lepcha and Bhutia dialects, and he recognised several words that were familiar to him.

That sense of helplessness became maddening, now that one of their number had been struck down. Never in his life had Bill Gresham felt so completely futile. He tried to gather all his strength together, so that he could at least move the electric torch, but his limbs refused to answer to the call of his brain.

A sound smote his ears. . . .

Throbbing on the air, weird and mysterious, came a sobbing wail. It was an unearthly, terrifying sound, and from the moment of its inception it increased rapidly in volume until it was echoing and re-echoing like the shrieks of souls in torment down the tunnel. Greater and greater grew the intensity, and the rock walls sent the sounds crashing to and fro in a veritable cataclysm of tumult.

The Tunnel Men stiffened. They cast furtive

glances at one another, and they stared uneasily along the tunnel—towards the exit, past Bill and his companions. Then they retreated, backing slowly at first, as though with reluctance. They grew more and more indistinct, until their shapes could no longer be seen . . . only their luminously glowing eyes.

Bill felt his muscles relaxing. Power was returning to his limbs. It was like a current being switched off. The paralysis vanished, and he was able to swing his torchlight round. To his relief, Peter was staggering to his feet.

" Hurt? " jerked Bill sharply.

" No," gasped Peter. " Not now. I . . . I don't seem to remember. . . ." He looked past Bill up the tunnel. " What was that awful sound?"

" Something which saved us from those rum-looking devils, anyway," replied Bill briskly. " The funny thing is, it came from *behind* us— from the exit. And that's our way out."

They looked at one another. The dread sounds had died throbbingly away, and now the tunnel was filled with an uncanny silence . . . a silence almost as terrifying as the unnatural sound had been. Even Big Bill himself, most reckless of adventurers, was somehow reluctant to go back along the tunnel.

" Whatever it is, it's up this way," he muttered gruffly. " Let's carry on in the other direction."

He felt that it was sheer folly to do so, but the temptation was too strong. Or perhaps—although he would never have admitted it—he was experiencing something akin to fear for the first time in his life. There is always something fearful in the Unknown, and that dreadful sound had come from the direction of the tunnel entrance. In spite of himself, Bill pictured some unthinkable monster on their scent.

A hundred yards, perhaps, they advanced. Then, unexpectedly, the tunnel widened out into a respectable-sized cavern. Big Bill switched off his light with a sharp exclamation. For the cavern was lighted quite independently of his feeble torch-beam.

" Phew!" breathed Peter.

They could see the sloping rock walls and a continuation of the tunnel some distance to their left, but not exactly opposite. The very centre of the cavern was occupied by a cone-like projection of rock, which rose from the floor to a height of fifteen or twenty feet.

" Ye gods! Look at that," said Bill strangely.

The rock, reddish in colour, streaked with orange and green, was as smooth as glass to a height of a dozen feet or a little more. But above that point the rocks were sharp and jagged and quite unworn.

" What do you make of it, skipper?" asked Reggie in a low voice.

" Looks as though some huge animals have been in the practice of rubbing themselves against the rock until they've worn it. . . ."

" Huge animals?" interrupted Reggie, with a start. " I say, how about getting out of this? Dash it, I'm not a nervous chap, but this place fairly gives me the willies!"

Bill Gresham pointed.

" We've got to have a look up there," he replied. " That's where the light's coming from. Can't you see how it streams upwards, and is then reflected from the roof?"

He was a fellow of action. He climbed unceremoniously upon Peter's sturdy shoulders, and, reaching upwards, was just able to grasp a projection of the rock where it ceased to be smooth. He hauled himself up, and then gave a hand to Peter, who had climbed on Reggie's shoulders.

Soon they were all three at the summit of the cone, staring at a jagged opening, twenty feet across, which yawned before them.

Hardly knowing what to expect, they went forward on hands and knees—cautiously, for the rocks were sharp and rough and treacherous. They did not wish to risk a stumble. Big Bill was the first to reach the edge, and he peered over. . . .

And his very senses deserted him, for the thing he saw was almost unbelievable.

Chapter Five

THE WORLD WITHIN
THE MOUNTAIN

BILL GRESHAM found himself looking straight down upon a vast panorama, a scene which spread itself out for *miles* in every direction. The air was crystal clear and full of a bright sun-like glow. Right beneath him was an immense, incredible drop. Two thousand feet sheer, if an inch. . . .

Two thousand feet!

And down below a world of its own . . . a world of trees and fields and rivers and, yes, human habitations! Houses. . . . Wooden houses. . . . Brick houses. . . .

" Kick me, somebody," said Big Bill angrily. " Either I'm stark mad or I'm dreaming—and a kick will do me good in either case."

But neither Reggie nor Peter kicked him. They wanted somebody to kick *them*. They were speechless. They were incapable of action. They were staring down, too, and they were seeing exactly the same things.

The sight was not as novel to them as it might have been to some, for they were experienced flyers, and they had the uncanny sensation that they were leaning out of a plane's cockpit, looking down upon a landscape thousands of feet below.

And they were doing exactly that very thing— looking down on a landscape thousands of feet below. It was like some freak fantasy, *for they knew that they were looking down into the very interior of mighty Mount Everest!* A small section of that interior, perhaps, but large enough, nevertheless, for them to discredit the evidence of their own eyes, to disbelieve their own senses.

The cavern they looked into from that hole in its roof was unlike any other cavern in the experience of mankind. From end to end it stretched for miles, and even at the sides the walls rose for hundreds of feet before sloping to join the roof. Big Bill and his comrades were peering down through this tiny hole in the centre of the roof. . . . The entire panorama, therefore, was spread out below them, and they could feel the warm, tranquil air flowing gently past them, upwards, carrying with it a smell of—life. They could not have put a name to the fragrance which assailed their nostrils, but it suggested something definite to their senses, something familiar and friendly.

" It's true, skipper," said Reggie Pickles, at last. " There's a world down here—right beneath us. A world that nobody on the earth we know has ever heard of. . . . Either that, dash it, or I'm just plain loopy!"

"Count me in," muttered Peter, his voice hoarse and strained. "A thing like this couldn't have been kept secret if any ordinary living human beings had seen it or heard of it. It's—it's just a dream!" He pointed, leaning perilously over in his excitement. "Look at those red-tiled roofs down there! And roads!"

"Who's got the glasses?" asked Bill. "Nobody, I suppose. What fools to forget them!"

He felt in his pockets helplessly. They had had field-glasses with them, but had jettisoned them with the cold-resisting suits and the oxygen helmets.

"It's all very well to glare at us, Bill, but how were we to know that we should need the glasses?" said Mustard defensively. "Perhaps we're better off without them, what? I mean, no chance of getting down into this Lost World. . . ."

"Be yourself, Reggie," interrupted Bill coolly. "Ye gods! Do you think we're going to let a thing like this slip up? There must be a way into this cavern, and we're going to find it."

"But we're right in the roof," protested Peter. "No earthly chance of getting down this way. We'd need miles of rope. . . ." He paused, blinking, for his senses still refused to accept the scene upon which he gazed. " We shall all wake up soon, of course!"

" Everything's impossible," jerked Reggie. " It's impossible that there can be people—real people—living in this impossible cavern. It's impossible that the cavern itself should be as light as day."

" It's just as impossible that there should be a tropically warm valley on the upper slopes of Everest," said Bill Gresham coolly. " We *know* the valley is a fact, because we've just come through it. It's just a question of adjusting our minds to something that had never entered into our calculations."

He fell silent—awed, perhaps, by the very magnitude of the facts his mind was called upon to grasp. And there was something else.... Was there a way into this Lost World? Equally important, *was there a way out?* If so, surely some of the people who lived in the unknown world would have made themselves known to civilisation —the other civilisation? It was a disturbing thought.

" H'm!" grunted Bill.

He looked again at that astonishing scene spread below him. Things which had not at first penetrated his intelligence now began to break through it.

" We're on Everest, don't forget—Mount Everest, in the Himalayas," he said deliberately, as though trying to convince himself of the fantastic fact. " On every side, wild country— mountains, foothills, plains. Tibetans . . . Mongolians on one side and Indians. . . . But look down here! Look at the houses, you chaps! Even without glasses I can see that some of the buildings are half-timbered and with twisted chimneys."

Reggie Pickles shook himself.

" Thanks, Bill," he said huskily. " You've just about saved my reason. I've been seeing these things, too, and I thought I was potty! I mean to say, where do you see such houses outside England? And the fields! Those square patches *are* fields, I suppose. All evenly cultivated. . . ."

" What are those dots moving along the roads?" asked Peter, almost feverishly. " They're people! And look. . . . I'll swear there's a farm cart, with horses pulling it. . . . And cattle in the meadows, too."

" Dash the cattle!" said Reggie. " What price this town immediately beneath us? Why, you can even distinguish the market square. . . . Yes, and there's a church spire. . . ."

" Listen!" interrupted Bill suddenly.

They jerked upright, dragging their attention away from the magical sight beneath, which was so near and yet so distant—dragging themselves back from this fantasy world into grim reality. The air was echoing with an awful throbbing wail, and it vibrated throughout the cavern. . . . The same sound as before, yet somehow different.

With one accord they scrambled down to the rock floor of the cavern. The uncertainty had got on their nerves. If there was danger to be met, they would meet it.

There was no time for further exploration. The mysterious menace of the tunnels had to be faced . . . and they had an overwhelming desire to get out into the open, under the sky they knew. A sense of being trapped was rapidly closing in on them.

Big Bill led the way into the tunnel, and they went racing along, retracing their steps. They only knew that they had to get out of this labyrinth of mystery. They ran hard, and all the time their ears were filled with a new and fearful sound. They reached the spot where they had encountered the Tunnel Men, but there was no living thing to be seen. Perspiring, breathing hard, they paused.

And a new phenomenon manifested itself.

Wind! A strong moist wind, ever increasing in

violence, was blowing down the tunnel, rushing past their faces and whistling in their ears.

"What's that?" yelled Reggie abruptly.

They stood stock-still, their hearts thudding like hammers. From somewhere just ahead of them came a terrific roaring, swishing sound. Bill's light snapped on. Something white, far up the tunnel, caught the beam—something which came charging onwards, stretching from one side of the tunnel to the other with relentless speed and force.

The next second they realised what it was—a veritable wall of water, foaming white, and hurtling along with irresistible ferocity.

Too late even to turn! The three comrades were picked up like straws and carried helplessly on the crest of the flood into the unknown depths.

Chapter Six

THE WHIRLPOOL

" GRAB hold!" roared Bill.

As cool as ice in the sudden terrible emergency, with only his head above the swirling foam, he flung out his two powerful hands. Reggie and Peter, in danger of being swept away from him, and from one another, seized those strong hands and held on.

" Don't know where we're going," yelled Bill, " but we're on our way!"

" Might as well stick together, what?" gurgled the irrepressible Reggie.

It was like Bill Gresham to speak flippantly in the face of stark danger. In that moment he and his comrades had every reason to believe that they were being swept along to certain death. The flood, hurtling down the mysterious tunnel, had caught them without warning.

To fight against it was impossible. It was as much as they could do to keep their heads above the surface. Mercifully, the level of the flood did not reach the tunnel roof, or they would have been drowned miserably.

Several illuminating thoughts flashed through

Bill's mind. Now he understood the meaning of the worn steps—worn, not by human feet, but by rushing water. Evidently this flooding of the tunnels was a periodic occurrence, something like the discharge of a geyser. . . .

Yes, and that explained the sobbing wail which had caused the Tunnel Men to bolt. They had known what the sound portended, for it was the warning that the water would soon come rushing down from the great void into which the outer cataracts poured.

" It can't be so deep, after all, if it overflows every now and again," said Bill. " Notice how tepid the water is? Not icy cold, as you'd expect, since it is obtained from the melting ice and snow."

" Who cares? " spluttered Peter.

" Perhaps you're right," admitted Bill. " Anyhow, the water must be heated somehow after it gets down into that ' bottomless ' pit."

Their speed increased alarmingly as the rushing water took a turn down a sloping section of the tunnel. They were jostled and spun about, and the creamy foam broke again and again over their heads. They found themselves shot into the cavern which they had left only a short time before—the farthest point of their exploration.

The glow of light from the cone-shaped projection in the floor enabled them to see clearly. They were swept towards the smooth rocks—and now it was clear why they *were* smooth up to a certain height—then on, and round in a dizzy half-circle. They could see the water swirling through a gap in the rocks—the continuation of the tunnel. They were carried into the opening as matches are carried down a flooded gutter.

" So long, boys," gasped Bill.

This, surely, was the end. The water surged over their heads and they were forced down and down as though giant hands were pressing them.

Half suffocated, clinging to one another desperately, they suddenly found their heads above water again, and they could see that they were being swept along a wider, deeper tunnel. As before, they could see the rock walls and the roof although there was no visible method of illumination.

" Look! " panted Peter.

For a fleeting second the others caught a glimpse of redly luminous spots near the top of the tunnel wall, beyond the reach of the flood water.

" Those rummy savages! " shouted Bill, as they passed. " By jove! Did you feel that shock just then? The beggars evidently ran down here and perched themselves on the ledge. It's a good sign."

" I don't believe in signs," said Peter gloomily.

" Isn't it clear that these periodic gushes can't last very long? Not that it really helps us very much. . . ."

The rest of Bill's words were literally engulfed, for the surging waters had closed over his head again. He thought he heard frantic shouts from his comrades, and at the same moment a feeling of nausea attacked the pit of his stomach.   He knew he was dropping—dropping sheer.

This must be the end. . . .

Even in that crucial moment Big Bill found himself thinking clearly. Reggie and Peter were still clutching at him and he was somehow comforted. Better that they shouldn't be separated . . .

Down. . . . down !

Bill had experienced this same ghastly sensation in a nightmare. But there was a difference. One awakened from a nightmare. . . . There would be no awakening from this horror.

His brain was vivid; his thoughts were as clearcut as quartz. They were dropping into another of those appalling chasms and it could only be a matter of seconds before . . .

Bill found himself drinking in a great gulp of air. Amid an incredible lather of foam the friends were being tossed up and down, and round and round, on giant waves. Bill opened his eyes and was surprised to find that he could dimly see his surroundings.

They were in a cavity of the mountain which was, in fact, an irregular-shaped grotto. Large at the base, its walls converged towards the top until it became narrow, like the neck of a funnel. Through this neck the water was pouring in a tumultous cascade.

Bill and his companions had been tossed into the great pool unharmed, and now they were being whirled round the outer edge of the immense body of water. They were all strong swimmers and they found it possible to keep their heads above the surface with comparative ease.

" Not dead yet!" bawled Big Bill.

But his words were wasted. The noise of the falling water in that hollow cavern, with its deafening echoes, was stupendous. The sounds beat upon their ears until their drums sang with sickening agony. They were on the opposite side of the rock basin now, and they could see the waterfall down which they had plunged. It was not in dead-centre, but at the side. The drop wasn't much; they must have fallen the distance in about three seconds. But it had seemed to them like three minutes.

The strength of the current, which was moving in circles, was so great that any attempt to swim against it was futile. Inexorably they were swept round until they plunged into the turmoil of water at the foot of the fall—like corks in a bath, sucked beneath a running tap. Under they went, tossing about, twisting and turning.

Gasping for breath they came bobbing to the surface again, only to find themselves being hurtled round on the same circuit. But this time they were nearer the centre of the pool. . . .

Thus, when they were again swept beneath the waterfall, its full force did not reach them. They were tossed about for a moment and then they were past. And for the first time Big Bill Gresham realised just what their fate was to be. Strong as his nerves were, he felt himself go limp and a sudden sickness assailed him.

Reggie and Peter were still close; he could see their faces, pale and drawn. He could see them staring down the sloping side of the vortex towards its centre. Here, half-way down the side of the whirlpool, the water was as smooth as glass, and moving with ever-increasing speed. Bill found himself staring at the pool's centre—fascinated, horrified.

A subterranean maelstrom!

He saw a circular hole in the water, about six feet across, and from that space came, like a giant's voice, a horrid gurgling and sucking. The thing was, literally, an immense plug-hole!

Once they were drawn into that all hope would indeed be lost, for the very suction itself would drag the life out of them.

The desire to keep on living was strong within Big Bill's virile mind. He shook himself grimly and made an attempt to swim. He laughed with bitterness. Useless. It was like trying to swim against the whirlpool rapids of Niagara. The force of the current was staggering.

There were still a few minutes. . . . The apparently doomed three were now being carried round in comparative smoothness. Before long the speed would increase—after they had been drawn farther down. And then they would spin like tops, to be finally sucked into that ghastly " plug-hole."

"All up, you chaps, I'm afraid," bellowed Lord Gresham. " Might as well take it on the chin. Can you hear me?"

"Just!" shouted Reggie. " I say, this is a mess!"

" Afraid so, old son."

" Just one of those things," roared Reggie.

Bill's heart went out to him. Not a word of complaint—as he had expected. He glanced at Peter—and Peter was floundering about almost helplessly, and there was a dazed look on his face.

" Who did that?" he gasped indignantly.

" Did what?"

" Something hit me!" bawled Peter, applying a dripping hand to his head, and shaking himself. " What's the idea of whacking a chap over the head like that?"

Big Bill only partially heard the words. But a moment later he understood perfectly. . . . Something unseen came out of the gloom and struck him a violent blow in the face. The pain, for the moment, was intense, and he was partially stunned. Something warm was trickling down his chin, and he knew that his nose was bleeding profusely.

He stared into the gloomy vault of the grotto. Above and on all sides he could see the rocks. Even in that critical moment he felt that it was all wrong. . . . He should never have been able to see the rocks. This place should have been a pit of inky darkness, ten times more terrifying still.

And then Bill Gresham—saw.

" Jumping kangaroos!" he yelled, employing an expression he had not used since his schooldays. " Look up there, you fellows! There—and there—and there!"

" Cheese it, Bill," protested Peter, distressed.

" Fathead! There may be a chance for us. . . ."

" Don't, skipper," panted Reggie Pickles. " It's only a matter of minutes now before . . ."

" Idiot!" bellowed Bill. " Can't you see the ropes?"

" Ropes!"

" A dozen of them—all hanging down, and some of them touching the water. One of them hit me just now. If we can't grab a rope each, and shin up it, then we deserve to go down the waste pipe!"

Bill's naturally high spirits soared. He fairly shouted with joy. When death had seemed inevitable, this unique way of escape had presented itself. It was almost like a miracle.

Bill's great strong hands grabbed at one of the long ropes as he was being carried swiftly beneath it; his fingers closed in a steel-like grip, and the jerk was so sudden that he felt that his arms were being dragged out of their sockets. But he held on. . . .

His progress was halted and he swung there at the end of the rope, the water swirling furiously about his middle, as though angry to lose its victim. Hand over hand, Bill pulled himself upwards, until he was free of the flood.

He wasted no time on wondering why the ropes were hanging so conveniently. He had eyes for nothing but his comrades. He saw Reggie grab at one of the ropes and hold on. Peter Fraser reached for another, missed, and plunged beneath the surface. He came up again, struggling and gasping.

Like a monkey Big Bill lowered himself on his rope, and reached out, hand extended—to grasp Peter when the latter should be whirled beneath him. But Peter succeeded in seizing a rope of his own and he pulled himself clear of the deadly whirlpool.

Safe for the moment! But what lay in store?

Chapter Seven

THE BIG DECISION

CLIMBING up with the energy of young muscles and perfect health, Lord William Everard Cornwallis Gresham was the first to find his feet on solid rock once again.

His rope—which was a real rope, if crudely made—was attached to an immense metal stake at the top of the cavern, where it was driven deeply into the rock. There was a ledge here—a ledge about three feet wide, running along the face of the cavern wall. Easy enough for Big Bill to get his feet on to it and balance himself.

He stared anxiously into the void.

Reggie Pickles was climbing steadily and strongly, and reached the ledge some twenty feet from the spot where Bill was standing. Peter Fraser, although actually bigger and stronger than Reggie, was the more exhausted—perhaps because of the head-blow he had received—and he was making hard work of the climb.

Bill's anxiety increased. He was helpless. He could do nothing—and twice Peter had slipped dangerously. The rope to which he was clinging was fastened to the opposite side of the cavern roof.

" He'll never make it," muttered Bill huskily.

He ran recklessly along the ledge. Perhaps he wasn't so helpless, after all. . . . It had just occurred to him that the ledge might continue all the way round—or, rather, it might zigzag about, for the shape of the grotto's roof was far from round. There was one spot where Bill was compelled to make a leap for it and he never gave a thought for the danger.

Over the gap he soared—and just made it. On the other side the ledge was wider. He ran fleetly and was just in time to give Peter a helping hand when it was most needed. Peter was desperately trying to grasp at the rock ledge, and he would never have succeeded. His leader's strong hands reached down, seized him, and pulled him to safety.

" Okay now, old son," said Bill. " Phew! That was a close call!"

" Thanks," muttered Peter. " Made a muck of it, didn't I? That crack on the head . . ."

" Forget it," interrupted Bill. " Take it easy for a bit."

He saw Reggie coming towards him. Reggie had found that the rock ledge continued the other way, and he was thus able to join his friends without indulging in the suicide jump. He had some news.

" I say, I came right under the falling water," he said excitedly. " And what do you think?"

" Is this a time for asking riddles, Mustard?"

" Sorry! But I'm dashed if there aren't more steps hewn in the rock—right underneath the water," said Reggie, his eyes glowing. " A bit rummy, what?"

" Well, one thing's certain," replied Big Bill thoughtfully. " The people who live in the Lost World—which we glimpsed not long ago—know all about this exit on to the upper slopes of Everest. I imagine that some of them must have been swept to death in this ghastly place—caught, probably, by the sudden rush of water down the tunnel, just as we were caught."

" You mean, these ropes . . ."

" Of course. These people fixed up the hanging ropes, to be used in case of emergency. Anybody caught napping, in that case, could grab a rope and haul himself to safety. Easier for them than for us—because they know the ropes are there."

" Yes," agreed Mustard. " We didn't know about them until it was almost too late." He breathed hard. " I still can't quite believe, you know, that I'm alive! That frightful current . . ." I say! Look down there!" He stared at the whirlpool. " It doesn't seem to be so frightful as I had supposed."

" The level has fallen," said Big Bill. " And the volume of falling water is less than half. The overflow period must be nearly over. . . . I say, do you fellows realise that the flood has only lasted about ten minutes?"

" You mean ten hours," growled Peter.

They could hear one another distinctly now. The tumult of noise was rapidly subsiding. Even as they watched, the gushing column of water dwindled to a mere trickle and then stopped altogether. Below, the flood rapidly sank lower and lower; until, with a sound of weird gurgling the last foaming smother vanished. And almost complete silence followed.

" Well, that's that," said Bill Gresham grimly. " We're getting out of here—quick. It may be days before the next ' period ' comes, or it may be half an hour. We're taking no chances. We've had enough excitement for a spell and now we'll take a rest."

The others did not argue. Throughout the arduous, perilous ascent of Everest they had obeyed Big Bill without question. Not only was he a capable leader, and probably the most expert mountain climber in the world, but he had a knack of commanding instant obedience from his comrades, and this without a word of actual command. Everything that Bill Gresham did was right.

They passed along the ledge, reached the rock steps, and climbed into the tunnel—which, but a few minutes earlier, had been filled with rushing water. It now contained a mere trickle. They walked quickly, the rocky sides and roof being visible to them—and yet they did not understand why they saw. At one place they came to a fork, where another tunnel joined this one. Reggie Pickles would have paused, but Bill would not agree.

" No," he said firmly. " We're getting out."

He was on the alert for any further sign of the Tunnel Men, but nothing was seen. Bill had no desire to taste another sample of that strange " electric paralysis " (as he thought of it for want of a better term). He had his own ideas, and with characteristic determination he meant to put them into immediate practice.

Hurrying on, it seemed an interminable journey, and more than once they feared they had lost their way, and were wandering aimlessly in the strange subterranean labyrinth. But at last, and with great relief, they reached the exit. Everything was as before; the ice-cold water of the melted snows was shooting down into the great void—or geyser-pool, as it apparently was. They climbed the rocks steps, emerged into the open, and breathed freely and thankfully.

" Well, I never expected to see daylight again," said Peter, who looked badly shaken. " And where do we stand now, skipper?" He stared up at the mist-enshrouded heights. " Ye gods and little fishes! Look at the slopes of ice disappearing into the clouds! There's no way out of this million-year-old crater. So far as getting back to our base camp is concerned we might as well be dead."

Young Lord Gresham made no comment. He was staring up at the slopes himself—and beyond, where the rocks became covered with snow, and where the snow turned to glassy ice. No, there was no possible way of getting out. He knew it. *But he wasn't thinking of getting out. . . .*

He was thinking of that Lost World in the heart of Everest. He had only emerged into the open again because it was a necessary step.

" Those cold-resisting suits," he said dreamily. " They're made of special rubber. . . . It's my hunch, you fellows, that the mysterious Tunnel Men are charged with some kind of electric force— due, perhaps, to their peculiar environment. Anyhow, the rubber suits may protect us. We shall see. The oxygen gear, too. . . ."

" To say nothing of grub," interrupted Reggie,

brightening. " Gad, I've just remembered. Our supply of rations is untouched."

Earlier, when they had shed their special suits, they had also shed packs, binoculars, and even the small automatic pistol which Bill Gresham had carried. Nobody had said a word about that automatic, but they all knew that the leader had carried it for use in a dire emergency—in short, to put an end to their lives should they have become hopelessly trapped in an ice crevice, with nothing but slow death staring them in the face.

They went back through the moist, gloomy wood, and then climbed the rocky slopes to the snow-line. Their discarded gear was just as they had left it.

Their meal was a frugal one, but their " iron rations " consisted of highly concentrated and nutritious foods, and they needed very little to give them fresh strength. Having donned their rubber suits and packs, they also carried the oxygen gear. At Big Bill's suggestion they had rested for a full hour, and now felt all the better for it.

" It seems to me there's one chance," said Bill quietly. " This is a one-way street, you fellows."

He indicated the glassy ice slopes stretching mysteriously into the upper mists.

" No hope of getting back *that* way," agreed Peter soberly.

" So we either stay here until we starve, or we make a shot at getting down into the extraordinary inner world," said Bill. " Not much choice, eh?"

" But, dash it, what about Bobby Simson and our pals at the Base Camp?" protested Reggie. " Surely we ought to do a spot of waiting, Bill! Bobby is bound to report that he's lost all sight of us. . . ."

" And then?"

" Then they'll come out scouting," replied Reggie brightly. " If we stick around, Bobby might even break through the storm clouds and spot us. Oughtn't we to give him a chance? We might even light fires. . . . Smoke signals, if you get the idea."

" Sorry, old son, but that's just wishful thinking," said Big Bill, shaking his head. " There's not a chance in five hundred million that Bobby's plane could ever break through the eternal hurricane that's raging up there." He looked at the storm-racked clouds. " If he tried to get through, his bus would be smashed to fragments."

Reggie nodded silently. He was remembering their foot-by-foot struggle against the ferocious blizzard as they had climbed the outer slopes. No plane would dare to come within a mile of the danger zone. . . . No plane, in their own expedition or any other, had ever caught a glimpse of this amazing valley—which was why it had remained undiscovered.

" Yes, I suppose you're right, Bill," said Reggie, his expression becoming more serious. " Might as well give up all hope of the plane finding us. But couldn't we explore this basin? Perhaps there's a way out. . . ."

" A waste of time," interrupted Bill, almost impatiently. " Look for yourself. The ice slopes, as steep as the roof of a house, and unclimbable, extend round the entire basin. We're like black beetles in an enamel pail—the more we try to get out, the more we shall exhaust ourselves by slipping back."

" Well, then, what about a rescue party?" persisted Reggie, who refused to give up hope. " They're bound to send out a rescue party from the Base Camp. . . ."

" Which is exactly what I'm thinking, too," nodded Bill calmly. " It'll take days to organise the party, and it'll take weeks before it can get anywhere near this elevation of the mountain. . . . Which gives us heaps of time, my sons, to explore the mysterious Lost World."

" There's awful danger in those tunnels. . . ." began Peter.

" Since when were you afraid of danger, ass?"

" We might never come out alive. . . ."

" That's true, but think of the excitement!"

" It's practically suicide. . . ."

" And think of the boredom, sitting here for days and weeks, waiting for the search party," continued Bill, with a grin. " My dear chaps, the decision makes itself. There's no choice. We've just *got* to find out the truth of the Tunnel Men and the secret of the Lost World."

Chapter Eight

THE GROTTO OF GOLDEN LIGHT

REGGIE PICKLES and Peter Fraser said no more. The decision, as Bill Gresham had pointed out, was self-made. A return to the interior of the mountain was the only course to be taken.

So back they went on their own tracks; back through the mysterious tunnels. New ground was reached when they came to the fork where Reggie had paused with the desire to explore. One tunnel led, as they knew, to the " plug-hole " cavern, and the other . . .?

The other rose sharply at the point where it branched, so sharply that a number of steps had to be climbed. This rise explained why the periodic flood never took the route. So the comrades took it. Soon they found themselves marching down a gradual descent which seemed to be everlasting. The tunnel was straight and true, and it made its way down and down into the very heart of the mountain. In places it widened, and in other places it narrowed, but in the main it kept a good average and never turned.

The air was pure; the young explorers could feel a soft, gentle current fanning their cheeks. At

first their feelings were charged with tense expec-
tancy, but after a while they became calmer. The
endless tunnel, in fact, was monotonous. There
was no branch, no opening of any kind in the rock
walls; nothing but the straight downward slope.

Just as they were beginning to think that they
would have to walk for hours, an abrupt change
came. An unexpected turn of the tunnel revealed
a golden glow some distance ahead. They hurried
their footsteps and, presently, paused in sheer
wonder.

They were on the threshold of an immensely
spacious grotto—actually, a lofty cavern. But it
was totally different from anything they had yet
encountered.

" What's this?" asked Reggie, wonderingly.
" Fairyland?"

The others ignored the flippant inquiry. The
scene before them was bewilderingly beautiful.
Suspended from the roof of the grotto were thousands of stalactites of every shape and size; and
the extraordinary thing was that each stalactite
glowed with an inner sunlight-like luminosity. The
floor of the grotto, stretching for hundreds of feet,
was similarly covered with numerous stalagmites,
which rose like shimmering sentinels. The whole
place was filled with the beautiful light, which
emanated from the very heart of the rock.

" Mystery No. 1 explained," said Bill Gresham cheerfully. " See how the rock itself is filled with light? Now we know why we could see our way along the tunnels."

" You may know," said Reggie. " I don't!"

" My dear chap, it's simple," said Big Bill. " There's a certain phosphorescent quality in the rock. Perhaps it's radio active. Here, in these stalactites, we see it in full blast, so to speak. In the tunnels it is present just the same—but only in small quantities. We could see the tunnel walls and roof, but we couldn't understand why."

" Gosh, I wonder if those beastly Tunnel Men have their bodies charged with electricity from the stuff?" asked Peter. " If so, that would explain why we got such a shock when they came near us."

Bill advanced to one of the great stalagmites which towered up to a height of eight or nine feet. At close quarters the glow was intense, but in no way distressing to the eyes. Bill touched it with his rubber-gloved hand, and felt nothing. He withdrew the glove and touched it with his bare fingers. The rock was cold, but it seemed to him that he had made contact with some live electric wires.

" That's useful," he said, with satisfaction. " The emanation is electrical, and rubber pro-

vides a perfect insulation. Next time we meet the
Tunnel Johnnies we shall be in better shape to
deal with them. Electrically charged rock, eh?
You can feel a kind of quiver in the very air, can't
you?''

They walked slowly towards the centre of the
great grotto, fascinated by the spectacle, picking
their way in between the numerous pillars of light-
giving rock.

'' Look! '' muttered Peter, pointing.

The centre of the grotto was an open space where
the rock floor was smooth and worn, as though
thousands of feet, over endless years, had trodden
there. In the very centre was a great pool, and
the water was so utterly still that it looked exactly
like a black mirror. It was difficult to believe that
it could actually be water.

The chums moved nearer, and stood at the edge,
gazing down at the glossy surface. The overhead
stalactites were reflected with amazingly stereo-
scopic clarity. The three young explorers felt that
they were not looking upon the surface of a pool,
but into another and even more amazing grotto.
The golden-glowing stalactites were now quite
different. In the pool they glowed, but not with
a golden light. They shimmered with every conceivable colour of the rainbow, winking and
twinkling as though endowed with life.

" By Jove!" muttered Big Bill, breathless.

He bent farther over and looked at his own reflection. It gave him something of a start, for it seemed that some entirely new and novel person was looking at him. His reflected image in the pool had depth and roundness, and, like the stalactites, the image glowed with endless colours after the fashion of shot silk. He moved a hand and the reflected hand left a rainbow trail of colours.

" Must be something in the water—if it *is* water," said Peter, in an awed voice. " Let's see."

He picked up a loose fragment of rock and tossed it into the centre of the pool. The rock plunged in with scarcely a sound—scarcely a splash. Only a number of lazy oily ripples slowly spread to the pool's outer edges. And the undulations were alive with liquid fire.

" It's water, but there's something mighty funny about it," said Bill Gresham. " See how quickly the ripples are subsiding. . . . Why, it's glassily still again. I've a good mind to put my hand in. . . ."

He broke off abruptly and his heart almost missed a beat. For, staring down upon that mirror-like surface, he had seen something which gave him more than a jolt. All the reflections were there, just the same—the stalactites and the three bending human forms. But while he had been speaking other forms had added themselves to the picture.

Human forms—ten of them—twenty—thirty! They appeared as though from nowhere, reflections of hideous-looking Tunnel Men.

Big Bill spun round, his hand leaping for his gun.

" Boys," said Bill steadily, " we've got company."

The grotto was completely filled with Tunnel Men!

Chapter Nine

THE MONSTER OF
THE POOL

THE coming of the mysterious denizens of the tunnel had been as silent as it was unaccountable. Not a sound had reached the ears of the three young explorers. One moment they had the grotto to themselves, and the next it seemed they were surrounded. While their attention had been diverted by the strange beauty of the pool, their enemies had acted.

There was no possibility of making a run for safety. From every corner of the grotto the Tunnel Men came closing in, appearing from behind the stalagmites as though by magic. The wide central open space was already filled; solid masses of the creatures stood silent and menacing. And behind Lord Bill Gresham and his companions was the pool. No escape that way.

" Heck ! " muttered Bill.

He was annoyed. He hated being caught napping. In spite of the peril of the situation he remained as cool as ice, and his brain acted like lightning. He could see in the first second that they had no chance of making a fight for it. They were outnumbered twenty to one.

" This looks nasty, boys," he whispered, and his lips scarcely moved. " Pretend to be paralysed. It might help."

Reggie and Peter heard, and understood. They remembered their previous encounter with these strange creatures; they remembered how they had been struck helpless. But now there was a difference. . . . Their rubber suits protected them, for they felt no paralysis whatever. *But the Tunnel Men did not know this!* It gave the chums a definite advantage.

Big Bill himself, acting on his own suggestion, had gone suddenly stiff, with one hand to a pocket and the other hand half pointing, his body slightly bent. He stood there rigid, his head partially turned towards his companions. He seemed to be utterly stricken; and he noted with satisfaction that Reggie and Peter had followed his example.

They waited, tense and breathless.

In the golden glow the strange creatures were even more hideous than the comrades had believed. The yellowish-white of their skins, so dead looking, was repulsive and unnatural. Their faces were cruel and savage, and their eyes, no longer luminous, appeared black and evil, like snake's eyes. As silently as before, the Tunnel Men came nearer and nearer—cautiously, as though they themselves were half afraid.

Not a move came from Big Bill. Reggie and Peter waited for him to act. They relied on him always.

The tension was eased when one of the savages, a leader of sorts, judging by his headgear, raised a hand and uttered a single cry. Instantly all movement ceased. The other Tunnel Men wore their dead-white hair in untidy mops, but this man had allowed his hair to grow longer, and it was so fashioned and stiffened that it resembled a gigantic hat.

The leader repeated the cry, and it was a signal, or command; for all the others raised their hands above their heads and faced the pool. From their throats came a long-drawn wailing cry. The sound rose higher and higher, echoing and re-echoing into the farthest corners of the great grotto. The sound rose to a shrill pitch, and then gradually died away as it had started.

It was a terrible cry, and Big Bill wondered what it portended. He deemed that the moment for action had not yet arrived. Moreover, he was curious, and his natural recklessness led him to hang on. He wanted to see what was going to happen.

He soon saw!

Out of the corner of his eye he glimpsed ripples appearing on the pool's surface; they became larger and larger, until little waves splashed against the rock edges; and each wave, as it broke, sent forth rainbow flashes of fire. Even more agitated became the pool's surface. Something huge, something *alive,* was rising to the surface— answering that call!

It was as much as Big Bill could do to hold himself rigid. He saw that Peter had moved slightly, and was glad that the Tunnel Men had not noticed. Peter could not be blamed. He had " gone stiff " with his back towards the pool and the desire to see what was happening behind him was irresistible. He slightly turned his head, and that move might have had serious results.

" Good gad!" came a horrified whisper from Reggie.

There was reason enough for his involuntary exclamation. The surface of the pool had broken in the centre, and a monstrous head rose slowly and menacingly into the golden glow. Higher and higher it towered, a head with coarse scales and a mouth which was literally as big as a steam shovel.

It was a monstrosity such as one dreams of in a nightmare. The eyes, saucer-like, were horribly dead looking. Up it towered, and its body was at least a dozen feet in diameter.

The Tunnel Men were now chanting rhythmically; the chorus was wailing and weird, but there was a certain lilt to it, and Big Bill saw that the monster of the pool was completely under control. Its very movements in rising out of the water were attuned to the rhythm of the chant.

Lord Gresham was a level-headed young man, and amazing though this experience was, he kept his wits fully about him. He was one of the least imaginative of souls—he was one hundred per cent practical—so he did not allow himself to regard this great creature as anything but normal —as Reggie and Peter undoubtedly did. He knew at once that it was a water snake. An extraordinarily large specimen, true, but nevertheless a species of snake. And Big Bill had never been afraid of snakes.

After the first shock of surprise, he felt even amused. Trying to scare him with a whacking great snake! It wasn't good enough, not by a long chalk.

At another signal from the leader, the Tunnel Men began closing in on the comrades. The monster was now slowly lowering itself back into the pool, its great jaws agape, revealing hideous fangs.

" Feeding time!" thought Bill grimly.

And he knew that he and his companions were to provide the three items on the menu. The thing was as obvious as daylight. It stuck out like a beacon. During those tense moments, however, Bill Gresham had been making good use of his eyes, and he had been particularly interested in a great stalactite which hung immediately over the pool. He glanced at it now, and wondered if it was as fragile as it looked. Much depended on that. . . .

It was a big stalactite, but at its base, where it was joined to the cavern roof, erosion had left only a string-like neck, by which it hung. Other stalactites were suspended by narrow necks of a similar kind, but none so precarious looking as this. Well, no harm in having a shot. . . .

He acted.

There was nothing else to be done, for the nearest savages were reaching out for him, even grasping him. But before they could take a firm hold Big Bill stepped briskly back and whipped the hand from his pocket. His fist contained his automatic pistol.

The Tunnel Men sprang back, startled by his move, for they had believed him to be helpless, as on that earlier occasion. A split second and the gun was pointing upwards and Bill squeezed the trigger. He was a dead shot, and his aim was true.

The bullet struck the neck of rock by which the gleaming stalactite hung. The result was staggering. Immediately following the sharp crack of the

report came a million flashes of fire from overhead. They sprang out from the grotto's roof like
flickers of lightning. Clearly, there was some
strange radio-active or electrical quality in the rock
which the impact of the bullet had detonated,
almost like an explosion.

The very air was suddenly charged with static
electricity, and the stalactite, shivering in all its
great bulk, parted company with the roof.

It fell sheer, and crashed down upon the head
of the monster of the pool.

Chapter Ten

INTO THE LOST WORLD

CHAOS immediately followed.

Big Bill and his comrades stood helpless, dazed spectators of what followed. For there was nothing they could do now. Bill, by his action, had precipitated an absolute cataclysm of movement.

Monster and stalactite both plunged beneath the pool's surface, and an enormous wave came cascading over, flooding the rocky edge and surging round the legs of the chums and rising almost to their knees. They were nauseated by a horribly fœtid stench, and at the same time a queer tingling sensation attacked them, even through the protection of their rubber suits. There was intense electricity, then, even in the water. Big Bill reached out a steadying hand and took hold of Reggie. The latter had been in danger of being sucked back into the pool by the receding wave.

Again the surface heaved, and for a moment the monstrous snake's head appeared, with a great gash where the stalactite had struck. The head rolled beneath the surface, and the inky-black water grew calmer.

"Seems to have done the trick," remarked Bill coolly.

The Tunnel Men had fled in all directions, and during the last few moments the grotto had been filled with their terrified screams. Obviously primitive, their stunted intelligence had been unable to grasp the nature of the thing that had happened. They only knew that their proposed victims had done something which was beyond their understanding—and thus they were afraid.

Before the pool was quiet every savage had gone. The young explorers had the grotto to themselves. Their astonishment was as great as their relief, for it seemed incredible that their numerous enemies could have vanished so quickly. There were two tunnels leading into the cavern—the one by which the comrades had entered and a smaller one on the other side. It was impossible that the hundreds of Tunnel Men could have escaped by these exits so quickly.

"The beggars aren't human," muttered Reggie huskily. "They couldn't have got away...."

"Simple enough," interrupted Bill, as practical as ever. "Come and look here."

They left the vicinity of the pool, and were glad to get away from it. Reggie and Peter, at least, knew that they had had an appallingly narrow escape. Only Big Bill treated the affair in a matter-of-fact way. He was walking now towards the nearest wall of the grotto, picking his way between the numerous stalagmites.

He pointed. And then, for the first time, the others saw hundreds of honeycomb-like holes in the cavern's side—holes so narrow and slit-like that it seemed impossible that any human being could have squeezed through.

Closer examination, however, proved that appearances were deceptive. There was room in plenty, and the holes led into narrow tunnels—which, unlike the main tunnels, were pitch black. The rock of which they were composed contained no scrap of the luminous ore.

" Not this way, thanks," said Bill, after penetrating a yard or two and returning. " In fact, the sooner we're out of this blighting place the better. Come on."

He led the way. Reggie and Peter were not short on courage, but they glanced at one another uneasily when they saw that their leader was making for the tunnel on the opposite side of the grotto. Their own inclination was to retreat by the way they had come. The farther they penetrated into this queer catacomb of unknown Everest the greater became the dangers.

" One bullet gone, and it was well spent," remarked Big Bill, patting the gun as he walked, and slipping it back into his pocket. " This looks like a continuation of the main artery. Jove! Look how it carries on straight into the mountain —as wide as a road and without a turn."

They walked briskly, and they walked steeply downhill. Now and again they glanced behind, half suspecting that the Tunnel Men would be following. But here was no sign of any living creature. They had the tunnel completely to themselves.

There was only one change. The air struck them more warmly and seemed fresher. Their rubber suits, designed for use in arctic cold, were now thoroughly uncomfortable.

" Better not shed them," advised Bill, as though he read the thoughts of his companions. " They protected us in the grotto, and they might protect us again. But for these suits we should have been a snake's dinner by this time."

" What's that glow ahead?" asked Peter suddenly. " Are we coming to another of these rummy grottoes?"

He was wrong. The tunnel ended abruptly, and they emerged upon a great rocky ledge as wide as a field. And ahead of him, for miles, stretched —space.

Space!

They had emerged, at last, into the Lost
World.

The young explorers stood transfixed with
wonder. The roof of the incredibly vast cavern
rose in dome-like majesty a thousand feet above
them. They stared at the staggering spectacle,
utterly speechless. They could hardly believe the
evidence of their own eyes. The very suddenness
of the panorama made them catch their breath.

The entire roof of the Lost World was covered
with a myriad luminous stalactites, which gave a
gentle, golden glow to the whole bewildering
scene. There was a radio-active property in the
light which was equivalent to sunshine. So far
above were the stalactites, so numerous were they,
that they were merged into one glowing " sky."

" I don't believe it!" gasped Reggie.

At first they thought they were on the floor of
the giant cavern. But they were wrong. Crossing
the wide space of rock, they mounted a curious
rampart, which seemed to be half-natural, half-
artificial, for at regular intervals there were loopholes—little tunnels in the rock.

" Wake me up, somebody," said Peter Fraser
faintly. " This isn't true, you chaps. We're in
our tent, dreaming! We're somewhere in Kampa
Dzong, and old Everest is in full sight ninety miles
away."

There was excellent reason for his remark. For they found themselves a thousand feet up the face of the mighty cavern wall, and below them stretched an amazing vista. The ledge, on either hand, ran round the face of the cliff as far as the eye could see. But they paid no attention to it now. . . .

They had eyes only for the panorama stretched straight ahead and below. Trees—real trees—fields and gently-flowing streams—pasture land, with grazing cattle! Immediately below, at the foot of the precipice, the nature of the ground was rocky and unfriendly, but farther out it quickly changed its character, becoming almost pastoral.

" Look," muttered Reggie, pointing. " As I live, farmhouses! And if those clustering buildings aren't thatched barns, I'm a Yogi! I've seen farms and outbuildings just like these in rural England."

" There's a village a mile or two away, over in this direction," said Peter breathlessly. " And look! Right in the middle of the landscape there's quite a town. We saw it from the hole in the roof. . . . Remember? Can't you see the church spires? I say, this is unbelievable!"

Big Bill Gresham laughed.

" What's the matter with you fellows?" he asked coolly. " That first glimpse prepared us for something like this, didn't it? Now perhaps you can understand why I was so determined to explore. How could we pass up a thrill like this? And don't keep saying you can't believe it—because it's hitting us smack in the face."

"Dash it, skipper, you're so dashed matter-of-fact," protested Reggie. "Nothing ever seems to get you rattled. . . . I mean, you're hardly human!"

Bill laughed again.

"It's only a question of adjusting your mind to unexpected conditions," he explained, with a chuckle. "I can adjust my mind in a minute and you fellows take weeks!" He leaned against the rock rampart and surveyed the scene interestedly. "There are people working in the fields over in this direction," he went on. "And isn't that a horse and trap jogging along the road down there? I can see a kind of suspension bridge. . . ."

He was human, after all. The awe-inspiring wonder of the scene bereft him of further words, and he fell silent. Like the others, he just stood staring. He was spellbound. For a moment his thoughts returned to their hundreds of miles of marching through Sikkim and the Himalayas to Tibet; he remembered their expedition toiling through the frontier passes of Kongra Is and Sebu La; he remembered the weary days of the first stages of the great climb, after Everest herself had been reached. . . . Somehow, Bill always thought of Everest as " her.". . . He found it difficult to believe that *this* was their objective; that they were actually within the heart of Everest.

But Bill's practical common sense revealed itself almost at once. While his comrades continued to stare at the scene below—so fascinated that they had not yet thought of using their binoculars—he gave his attention to what he saw on the ledge itself. And his quick brain " tumbled " to something which was grimly, even terribly, significant.

Without saying anything to the others, he climbed down from the rampart and examined the curious loopholes which had attracted his attention at first. He walked two or three hundred yards, and then back again. There were literally hundreds of the loopholes in this immediate vicinity. . . . And the ledge stretched for miles. Apparently there were thousands of the loopholes along the miles of rampart. . . .

" Just a minute, boys," he called abruptly.

Reggie and Peter joined him, startled by the grim tone of his voice.

" Something fishy about this," continued Bill, pointing. " Look here. What do you make of this?"

He plunged into one of the loopholes—a tunnel-like space in the rampart just big enough to accept his body. He emerged with a strange looking object . . . . a twelve-foot pole with a lot of vegetable fibre wrapped round it. At least, so it first appeared.

" What the dickens is it?" wondered Reggie.

" Unless my guess is wrong, it's a kind of primitive parasol or umbrella, of bloated dimensions," said Bill, significantly. " See, here are the staves, all joined together at the top. Hang on, Mustard. We'll soon see."

They struggled with the contraption and after a moment it opened out like a vast umbrella. It was nearly as big as a bell tent.

" You see?" said Bill coolly. " Big enough to carry an ordinary man—and to carry him safely, too."

" You're right," said Peter, staring. " It's crude and primitive, but it looks efficient enough. What do you make of it? What's it for, really?"

" I've been having a look round," said Bill Gresham deliberately. " There are thousands of these things, and they're all stuck, pole first, into the rock crevices. Take a look over the top of the rampart. . . . You can see the ends of the poles sticking out. That's what attracted my attention. . . . And against each primitive parachute, all nice and handy, there's a wicked looking bludgeon. And you may have noticed there's a current of air wafting *outwards* from the rock wall."

His chums stared rather blankly.

"But why?" asked Peter wonderingly. "I don't get it, Bill. What does it mean?"

"It means one thing or I'm missing my guess," retorted Bill grimly. "Our old pals, the Tunnel Men, are not so dumb as we thought. . . ."

"The Tunnel Men?" ejaculated Reggie.

"Who else? They must have been preparing for years—preparing to attack the inhabitants of the Lost World," said Bill, with conviction. "By the look of things they're nearly ready for The Day—for zero hour. Don't you get it, chaps?" His eyes were blazing. "Now we can understand why the beggars resented our coming—why they tried to throw us to the monster. They didn't want us to carry a preliminary warning. . . . We're white people, and the inhabitants of this great cavern must be white people, too."

Reggie and Peter were deeply impressed. Undoubtedly their leader was right. They saw the loopholes and the projecting "umbrellas," with a cruel bludgeon nearby. . . . These preparations, as Bill had said, must have been made in secret over a long period of time—perhaps years. The ledge, a thousand feet up the cliff face, was practically invisible to the inhabitants of the Lost World.

Which could mean only one thing. . . .

At a given signal—and a signal which was soon to come—thousands of the savages would take to the primitive parasols, and each savage would carry a bludgeon. Thus they would fall like a swarm of human locusts on the fair countryside below. The people of that peaceful land would have no warning—no time to prepare against the sudden overwhelming attack.

" This isn't merely amazing—it's mind-staggering," said Peter huskily. " These people— savages and whites alike—have been cut off from the rest of the world for goodness knows how many years—and here they are with their parachute troops!"

" Yes, it's a bit of a facer," admitted Bill. "We seem to have been sent by Providence. . . . We've arrived at a crucial hour. . . ."

" Talking about crucial hours," interrupted Reggie.

Bill turned and his jaw squared itself.

" Thanks, Reggie! These blighters are uncanny, aren't they?" he said grimly. " They come up like ghosts!"

For a moment Peter did not know what they were talking about. . . . Then he saw. The great ledge, in both directions, was swarming with Tunnel Men, and each savage carried a bludgeon. They had come up without a sound and they were advancing cautiously. But the instant they saw that they were observed, they made a mad rush.

" That's done it!" yelled Big Bill . " To face this tide would be death. We've got one chance. Quick! The parasols!"

It was touch and go, and only Bill's lightning decision saved them. He dived into one of the rock slits, and Reggie and Peter understood. They followed his example, and exactly as Bill had said they found a parasol lying ready—its pole, with a crook attached, projecting out into the open. It was a second's work to grasp the crook and leap into space.

Almost simultaneously the three chums launched themselves outwards, and from above came a wild chorus of maniacal fury. The outward leap carried the comrades well clear of the cliff, and for a moment they plunged down like falling stones, doubting if the crazy contrivances on which their lives depended would ever open.

But they did open—and with surprising efficiency. Clap—clap—clap! Almost in the same second the three parasols spread out, making a noise like a ship's sail struck by a squall. Reggie nearly lost his grip on the pole's crook, and was within an ace of plunging to his death.

" Okay?" shouted Big Bill coolly, as he floated some distance from the others. " That was a pretty near thing, but we've dished the beggars properly this time."

" Near thing?" gasped Reggie. " Has any-body seen one of my arms? It was jerked out of its socket a minute ago. . . . Good gad! I thought I was a goner!"

They floated down slantingly, oscillating gently from side to side as the air current carried them well out towards the centre of the Lost World. They were, in fact, being drifted straight down on to the central town.

Lower and lower!

It was really a beautiful, peaceful descent, for by now all sounds of the Tunnel Men had sub-sided. And presently other sounds came to the ears of the young explorers. They had been seen by the people on the ground below.

Figures were running across the fields and along the roads—all staring upwards, all shouting. With every moment that passed the excitement grew, and as the chums drifted straight over the town the streets became filled.

" Listen!" yelled Peter, in amazement.

He, like the others, had been fascinated by the

sight of the excited people in the streets of the town. But now he could hear the shouts of those people, and he could hardly believe his ears.

" See! They are white men!" came a cry.

" White men from the Outer World!"

" Heaven be praised!"

" At last—at last!"

These shouts, and many others like them, swelled into a mighty confusion of sounds. And the language was—English! That astonishing fact bewildered the comrades more than everything that had gone before. And this in spite of the fact that they had been prepared—for the very appearance of the landscape had impressed its English character on their minds.

Into the very heart of the central town dropped Bill Gresham and his stalwart comrades. Almost miraculously, they escaped colliding with the buildings, and fell into the streets; and as their feet touched ground they found themselves surrounded by wildly shouting throngs.

" Pleased to meet you," said Big Bill coolly. " We thought we'd drop in!"

Chapter Eleven

THE PEOPLE OF
THE CAVERN

CROWDS of people, mostly young men, came surging round the three astonished Everest climbers as they recovered their feet after landing. The parasol-like 'chutes were swept aside by the excited crowd.

"They are white!" went up the cry. "They speak our language!"

"They are from the great world beyond the snows!"

"'Tis a miracle!"

The shouting was so noisy that Bill Gresham found it difficult to make himself heard.

"Take it easy, brothers," he protested, laughing. "You're quite right—we're white, and we're British. . . . Here, I say. . . ."

The enthusiasm was reaching such a pitch that the three arrivals were literally swept off their feet and carried along by the human tide. Hands were stretched out to grasp theirs and the friendliness of the reception was beyond doubt, if embarrassing in its warmth.

"Welcome—welcome!"

The cry was taken up and continuously repeated. Unquestionably, these people of the Lost World were of British origin. They spoke English,

but it was an English which had a subtle difference
—due, of course, to the fact that the people had had
no contact with the outer world for a great number of years; exactly how many years Big Bill
could not guess.

" To the High Sheriff!" shouted somebody.

" Ay—ay!"

" To the Lord Renold!"

It was useless for Bill and his chums to protest.
They were on their feet again now, and they were
being hustled along the centre of a wide street, and
more and more people were adding to the throng.
Bright-eyed girls sprang forward and saluted the
comrades with kisses. And the shouting increased
until the whole town was in an uproar.

Children were appearing as from nowhere; they
came in sudden crowds, and Bill suspected that
they had been suddenly released from school.
Their excited shrieks of eagerness added to the
general confusion.

Bill had time to note that the men were dressed
in a curiously old-fashioned style; the material
from which their clothing was made was loosely
woven, the product of hand looms, and their open-
necked shirts were of coarse texture. The women
and girls were lightly dressed, to suit the perpet-
ually warm " climate " of the strange subterranean world, and the fashion was quaintly old-

world except for the fact that the skirts were nearly knee-high. Feminine instinct, apparently, permitted the women of the Lost World to keep abreast of the times!

Colours were lacking, and the clothing material for the most part was rather drab.

" Look! Shops!" shouted Reggie Pickles, pointing. " Good gad! This has got me beaten, skipper! Like a scene out of a Dickens book, what?"

The simile was apt. The half-timbered houses with their thatched roofs and oddly-shaped gables were reminiscent of a past age; and the low-fronted shops looked quaint indeed to the modern eyes of the visitors.

There were all the usual shops—drapers, butchers, grocers, bakers, etc.—and the majority of them carried picturesque signs, reminiscent of Old London. The names over the shops, however, were directly connected with the trades concerned, and this was so general that it could be no mere coincidence.

Over the baker's shop: " James Stuart Baker," over the butcher's shop: " Richard W. Butcher," over the draper's shop: " Bartholomew Draper," and so on. Bill was reminded of the McLeods and the McDonalds of Nova Scotia, who are so numerous that they are known mainly by

nicknames. Apparently there was an acute short-
age of surnames in this lost community.

A big square was reached, the centre of which
was evidently used as a market. Numbers of
wheeled stalls, containing all kinds of merchandise
and provisions, were being hastily pushed into the
side streets by the traders, in order to make room
for the advancing crowds. The excitement was
swelling greater and greater with every minute.

One building facing the square was considerably
bigger than all the rest, and along its front ran a
wide balcony on the first floor. Double windows
had just opened, and a tall, elderly man had
emerged, attended by several other men. He was
looking both startled and agitated, apparently at
a complete loss to account for the wild hysteria
which was sweeping through the town like a
forest fire.

" News, my lord—news! "

" Joyous tidings! "

The tall man maintained his dignity in spite of
his agitation, and he advanced to the front of the
balcony and held up a silencing hand. Instantly,
the tumult died away.

" What is happening? " he asked, in a grave,
almost stern voice.

" Joyous news, my lord! "

One man, evidently a person of some authority,

had advanced beyond the pressing crowd, beyond the comrades, and he stood beneath the balcony, his face flushed, his upturned eyes sparkling.

"We bring strangers, my lord," he announced, unable to contain his excitement, his voice swelling. "The first strangers to enter our domain within memory of living man!"

"Is this possible?"

"See, my lord! They are young men of fine build, if grotesquely attired, and they speak our own good English language!"

The tall elderly man leaned over the balcony.

"This is indeed an amazing event," he said, his voice quivering. "Bid them come to me."

During this brief pause Big Bill, as cool as ever, had made an interesting experiment. Removing his rubber gloves he touched the arms of the people who stood nearest; and he was relieved to find that there was no paralysing result. The people of the Great Cavern, then, were different from the Tunnel Men. They were, indeed, normal human beings.

"Might as well shed this gear, chaps," said Bill briskly, as he wriggled out of his rubber suit. "Can't expect 'em to appreciate us while we're lumbered up with all this truck."

"It's an idea," said Peter, following suit.

"One of you had better stop down here," added

Bill, becoming suddenly grave as he glanced up towards the vaguely distant, stalactite-studded " sky." " I can't help thinking of those brutes up there on the ledge. . . ."

Further talk was difficult, for he was more or less dragged into a wide doorway. Peter Fraser was with him, and they were escorted by a dozen enthusiastic stalwarts. Somehow or other, Reggie managed to make the people understand that he wanted to remain below, in the open square. And Reggie was keeping an alert eye on the " sky."

The shouting died down and a silence fell as Bill and Peter appeared on the balcony, face to face with the elderly man, who regarded them with kindly warmth.

" You are standing before the Lord Renold, the High Sheriff, the ruler of Lacuna," said one of the escort breathlessly. " My lord, the strangers— undoubtedly from the outer world—dropped un- expectedly upon us from the upper air, carried by strange and vast umbrellas."

That remark told Bill Gresham much, and his jaw instinctively tightened. The crude parachutes invented by the Tunnel Men, then, were complete- ly unfamiliar to the people of the Great Cavern! They were in absolute ignorance of the threatened attack—an attack which had probably been in active preparation for months, perhaps for years.

" There's no mystery, sir," said Big Bill, in his matter-of-fact way. " We climbed the mountain, fell into an extinct crater, found a tunnel, and the tunnel led us into this cavern. Pleased to meet you, Lord Renold. Gresham is the name—Bill Gresham. This is my friend, Peter Fraser, and my other friend, Reggie Pickles, is down in the square. We're members of the Gresham Everest Expedition, and we found rather more on Everest than we bargained for."

" You are actually—from England?"

" Is it so hard to believe, sir?"

" It is almost impossible to believe," replied the High Sheriff, with mingled wonder and joy, " You are from the great world—from England herself! This is indeed a great day for Lacuna."

" A great day for us, too," said Peter.

" Welcome, fellow men of England," said Lord Renold, his voice husky and vibrant. " You see in us the Lost People. For eighty-five years we have waited to greet you. Our fathers and our grandfathers were denied this joy. . . ."

" I get it," interrupted Big Bill briskly. " Your ancestors, then, were bottled up in this place eighty-five years ago, and since then you have been lost to the world." He wrinkled his forehead. " Renold. . . . I wonder if by any chance you can be a descendant of the celebrated Earl of Renold who fought so gallantly in the Indian Mutiny?"

"He was my grandfather," replied the High Sheriff quietly. "How wonderful—how glorious—to know that his name is still remembered. . ."

"If you don't mind, sir, we'll go into these details later," interrupted Bill Gresham. "There's something else—something of vital importance—to talk about now."

He was bursting with curiosity to know the facts of the Lost World—or Lacuna, as its inhabitants called it. But curiosity could wait.

"The point is this, sir," he continued, his manner urgent and brisk. "Do you know the actual strength of the Tunnel Men?"

The ruler of Lacuna was plainly puzzled, and so were those who stood about him—members of his council, no doubt, who were waiting to be introduced. Below, the massed crowds in the great square waited, too—patiently and expectantly.

"Perhaps the term 'Tunnel Men' doesn't mean anything to you," said Bill, seeing the mystification on Lord Renold's face. "That's only what we call the beggars."

"I confess, young friend, that I am completely puzzled by your words. . . ."

"Surely you know that there are lots of savages roaming about in the tunnels that lead to this cavern?'' interrupted Bill. '' We met some of them on the way. Ugly, shaggy brutes with queer eyes. . . .'' Lord Renold smiled.

'' You mean, doubtless, the Hillmen outcasts— the Jungas?'' he said with a shrug. '' They are indeed savage. In the earlier days of Lacuna these wretched people lived with us in the Great Cavern; but as their numbers increased more rapidly than our own they eventually became a menace.''

'' I can believe it,'' said Bill grimly.

'' They plundered and murdered,'' went on Lord Renold. '' And so, in self-defence, thirty-five years ago, we were compelled to banish them into the Lesser Cavern. The connecting tunnel blocked and since then our people have known peace.''

'' I see.''

Bill thought rapidly. The contempt in the High Sheriff's voice was unmistakable. One or two of the men with him, who were clearly under thirty years of age, were smiling sceptically, as one smiles who listens to a legend. They only knew of the Junga outcasts by hearsay.

'' You have known peace for thirty-five years,'' said Bill impressively. '' Well, my lord, I don't think you'll know peace much longer. You may have banished the Jungas, but you didn't destroy

them. By what I have seen they're dangerous, and
for years they've been planning to attack you."

He expected his warning to be greeted with
serious attention, but the Lord Renold smiled
broadly, and one or two of the others laughed out-
right.

" Your fears are groundless, young friend,"
said the High Sheriff gently. " At the best the
Jungas are degenerate half-castes, the descendants
of the original Lepcha and Bhutia hillmen who
were the servants of our forefathers. They are
ignorant and mentally negligible, and not to be
feared in any way. Our younger people, who were
born after the expulsion, scarcely believe in them
at all. In any case, there is no manner in which
they can reach this cavern, since the only tunnel
was blocked. . . ."

" Then you know nothing of the great ledge, a
thousand feet above?" asked Big Bill rapidly.
" The ledge that seems to encircle the entire
cavern? Man alive! This danger is imminent,
and it might fall on you any minute! The brutes
know that we have come among you, and it's any
odds they'll attack at once, whatever their original
plan may have been. Their whole object was to
catch you by surprise."

He saw the scepticism on the faces of his
listeners.

" Don't you understand?" he went on urgently. " Our coming has destroyed the surprise element. The Lepchas, or whatever you call them, will strike *now*, before you can organise any resistance."

Still that scepticism persisted—and was, indeed, augmented by annoyance and impatience. Impulsively, Bill turned and strode to the edge of the balcony, where he faced the throng and flung up a silencing hand.

" People of Lacuna!" he bellowed, his powerful voice carrying to the far ends of the square. " Prepare! The enemy will soon be upon you! Arm yourselves for the attack!"

For a moment there was a stunned silence; then the people moved restlessly and a murmur arose, gradually swelling to a hubbub of bewilderment. The High Sheriff, an angry frown appearing on his kindly face, moved forward to join Bill at the front of the balcony.

" What madness is this, stranger?" he asked sternly.

" I'm not trying to throw a scare into you," said Bill Gresham earnestly, after an anxious glance into the upper air. " Those infernal brutes may be coming down to attack you at any minute. For the love of Mike, arm yourselves! Not tomorrow—not next week—but *now*! Get ready to fight."

Chapter Twelve
A FEAST AND A STORY

THE hubbub in the crowded square increased, and the shouts which now arose contained an angry note. The people were no longer laughing, and there was an air of bewilderment—and even consternation—in their manner.

" Is this young man insane?" went up a shout, from somebody. " Why does he talk so strangely?"

The Lord Renold seized Bill Gresham firmly by the arm and drew him back to the rear of the balcony. The old man's face was sterner than ever.

" Your folly, young sir, is as great as your lack of respect," he said curtly. " We greet you in friendly spirit, and in return . . ."

" In return I do my utmost to impress on your people the danger that is imminent and grave," interrupted Big Bill swiftly.

The High Sheriff nodded and glanced significantly at the other men on the balcony. They understood at once, for they closed round Bill and Peter and forced them into an airy and comfortably furnished room. Lord Renold returned to the front of the balcony and held up his hand.

" We must be patient with our young friends from the Great World," he said, his voice sounding clearly in the silence which greeted his gesture. " It seems that they have encountered a few of the hairy Jungas on their way through the upper tunnels, and they imagine we are in danger. We must forgive them and make them welcome."

There was a moment of silence, a laugh, and then a cheer. A sort of sigh passed over the crowd, and the tension was over. In a moment or two the laughter increased, and the cheers grew louder and louder.

Lord Renold entered the room and closed the double windows, shutting out most of the tumult. The gravity had left his face, and he was looking slightly amused.

" Now, young friend, if you will tell me your story. . . . Oh, but wait. There is a third member of your party, I think? I would like to meet him."

Bill shrugged helplessly.

" I left Reggie down in the square so that he could keep his eye on the upper ledge," he explained. " The idea was for him to give a warning at the first sign of danger. . . ."

" There is no danger."

" You're wrong, sir, but I can see that I am wasting my breath," retorted Bill doggedly. " Perhaps I went to work in the wrong way. If so,

I apologise. You don't know what these Tunnel Men have been up to—what preparation they have made."

" I know, at least, that the Jungas are quite beneath contempt," said the High Sheriff, smiling. " Charles, perhaps you will go down and find our third visitor?"

One of the men nodded and left the room. In a few minutes he returned with Reggie Pickles.

" No sign of anything yet, Bill . . ." began Reggie.

" Let me introduce you to Lord Renold," interrupted Bill. " He says there's no danger, and for all I know he may be right. Lord Renold, this is my pal, Reggie Pickles."

There were more introductions. The dignified men with the High Sheriff appeared to be members of his Council. Apparently, the Council had been sitting at the time the chums had " dropped in."

The leisurely proceedings irritated Bill, and half-amused him, too. He fervently hoped that nothing would happen to jolt these good people out of their complacent inertia. They were so sceptical of any kind of danger that the High Sheriff even gave orders, then and there, for a great feast to be prepared in the Town Hall, so that the guests could be suitably welcomed and entertained.

Bill told his story briefly, in short, brisk sentences. There would be time for a fuller, more leisurely account when he had satisfied himself that his fears were groundless. His audience was greatly interested when he spoke of the dramatic flooding of the tunnel, and the escape from the whirlpool.

" Yes, the periodic gush of water is highly dangerous, I understand," said Lord Renold, nodding. "Our people found that out many years ago, and our engineers fixed the hanging ropes as a measure of safeguard. . . . You will have realised, of course, that it was our fathers who cut the crude steps out of the solid rock. In those earlier days there was always a hope that an escape to the outer world would be possible."

Bill told of their encounter with the Tunnel Men, and his audience appeared surprised and puzzled when he spoke of the savages' strange electrical emanations. It was obvious, in fact, that the story was received with plain scepticism. The Tunnel Men, or Jungas, were—in the eyes of these good people—little better than animals, and not to be feared in any way.

" How many of these unfortunate creatures did you encounter?" asked Lord Renold curiously.

" Quite a few. Perhaps fifty or sixty."

" Are we to be afraid of a wretched handful of

degenerate hillmen? I can quite understand your alarm. . . ."

" I don't think you do understand it, sir," said Bill grimly. " Although we encountered only fifty or sixty of the Jungas, we saw evidence of much larger numbers—evidence of active preparations for an air invasion of the Great Cavern. It is my firm conviction that the savages have been preparing for years. . . ."

" You speak of an ' air invasion ', young friend," put in one of the councillors. " I don't quite understand your meaning."

" They will descend upon you just as Peter and Reggie and I descended," explained Bill. " Only they will come in hundreds—perhaps thousands. We used three of their crude parachutes, and if we could drop safely in that way so can they."

The word " parachute " meant nothing to his hearers, so he explained more fully. He told of the hundreds of loopholes in the rock ramparts of the ledge a thousand feet up the cavern wall.

And while Bill was talking he was forced to the uneasy realisation that he had only seen a small number of these loopholes, and their prepared " parachutes " and bludgeons. He had taken the rest for granted. Perhaps his fear of a mass invasion was indeed a mere flight of fancy.

At any rate, the Lord Renold and his learned

councillors were in no way alarmed by Bill's story, and before long Bill himself was half convinced that he had been making a mountain out of a mole-hill. . . . But only half convinced. At the back of his mind a grim, ugly suspicion lurked and refused to be stilled.

However, there was nothing he could do about it. He and his chums were soon in a whirl of new excitements; they were taken here, there, and everywhere, and the whole town was in a fever of excitement and curiosity. It was so impossible to warn these good people of their possible danger that Bill gave it up as a bad job. He was comforted by the thought that the Jungas would have their own preparations to make, even if his fears were fully justified. It might take them days—and it would certainly take them hours—to gather their forces.

When the feast of welcome was over, and the initial excitement had died down, Bill might be able to get a more serious hearing, and there would still be time to awaken these people out of their complacency.

With Renoldtown—as this centrally-situated city was called—*en fête* there was no lack of interest for the comrades. Reggie and Peter completely forgot the existence of the Tunnel Men in this new and bewilderingly exciting experience.

Only the level-headed Bill continued to cast an occasional alert and uneasy glance at the " sky." Always at the back of his mind was the thought of —danger.

When the banquet finally took place, the chums were more or less paraded before the elite of Lacuna; they were introduced to the high ladies of the community and their daughters—and many of the latter were remarkably pretty and charming.

It was not until the feast was ended and they were sitting over some excellent wine, that the young adventurers heard what they had been burning to hear from the very start—the story of the Lucanians' origin. It was Bill's reference to the Tunnel Men—for the savages were still lurking in his mind—that broached the subject.

" The wretched hill tribesmen were always a problem," said the Lord Renold thoughtfully. " For many years they were a sore trial to our fathers. They were lazy, quarrelsome and cunning—but never dangerous. At first they were used as servants, the men as labourers and the women as hand-maids. But they were more trouble than they were worth."

He swept out a hand as though indicating the strange landscape beyond the Town Hall walls.

" Everything that you have seen here has been

done without the aid of the miserable Jungas. Thirty-five years ago, after a number of dastardly atrocities, the whole tribe, including the smallest child, was expelled to the Lesser Cavern."

" What is the Lesser Cavern?" asked Bill.

" It is perhaps half the size of this, and the lighting is much inferior," replied the High Sheriff. " Our fathers found that vegetation would grow there, but it was coarser. The cavern contains geysers and one or two dreadful crevices with volcanic fire. The fumes, however, find a natural outlet and do not pollute the general atmosphere. We had no compunction in driving the natives into the cavern and blocking the connecting tunnel."

" That was over thirty years ago," nodded Bill. " You didn't know it, but you did a rash thing. There's something in the other cavern which has strengthened the beggars. Radio-activity, I believe. They are positively charged with high voltage electricity. . . ." He broke off and smiled. " But perhaps I am fanciful, and I had better change the subject. How is it that vegetation can grow in this subterranean cavern, so far from the sun's power?"

" We do not understand it; our fathers did not understand it," replied the High Sheriff. " We only know that there is some quality in the glow from the roof which is akin to sunlight. Where you have seen fields and woods there was once nothing but tangled weeds and stones."

" It took a lot of cultivation, what?" asked Reggie.

" Many years were spent in cultivation. Our people when they first came here suffered untold privation and hunger, for food was difficult to pro-cure. For over twenty years it was a grim struggle —for very life. After that dreadful period came a rapid improvement. The soil began to produce plentiful crops. We were permitted, ultimately, to devote ourselves to other matters—to the build-ing of better habitations, to the planning of our towns, and so forth."

" What you say is extraordinarily interesting," said Bill, in wonder. " But I'm puzzled. How was it that your first people entered the cavern? And why? How was the cavern first dicovered?"

" It is a tragic story," replied the Lord Renold gravely. " A long story. . . Some other time. . ."

" Why not a thumbnail sketch now?" asked Bill.

" I can give you a brief account of our history, yes," said the other, smiling. " Our ancestors entered the cavern by sheer chance—as the result of an act of treachery which must be unequalled in India's history."

" In connection with the Indian Mutiny?"

" The Indian Mutiny is the beginning of our history," said the High Sheriff, nodding. " Naturally, we know nothing of what befell in Hindustan, where the mutiny actually raged, we know nothing of the outcome. . . . From that day to this we have had no communication with the outside world. You, in good time, will tell us. You will tell us who now sits upon the throne of England, in place of the great and good Queen Victoria. . . ."

" We're going to have a busy time," smiled Bill Gresham. " But please carry on."

" Carry on? Oh, you mean continue my story?" said the Lord Renold. " Well, when the Mutiny was at its height an eddy of the great upheaval penetrated to the isolated region of Sikkim. My grandfather, the Earl of Renold, was fighting against the mutinous Sepoys in Hindustan. My father was little more than a lad, and he was with the Norton family on holiday near the Himalayas. There were several British families—Major General Philip Norton, his wife and three children; Lieutenant Stuart Gresham and his young wife. . . ."

" Can you beat that!" said Big Bill, in wonder. " A relative of mine, I'll bet. In any case, one of the Gresham clan. It's a small world, after all."

" Then there was Dr. Evan Morgan and his family," continued the High Sheriff. " And others. . . . All this I know because it is written in our records."

" But how . . .?"

" You are impatient, young friend. The trouble began with a minor rebellion at the hill station to which I have already referred. The families I have mentioned, and some others, were compelled to flee northwards into the mountains. With them went a considerable number of native servants. They were joined later by Tibetan guides, who led them through grim mountain passes. At the head of this refugee band was a supposedly faithful fakir, a man who had served the British with steadfast loyalty. He had spoken of a big cavern, reached by tunnels in the mountain, where all would be temporarily safe."

" How large was the party?"

" It was very large. Many hundreds, in fact. In addition to the white men and their families there were native Sikkim servants and Tibetan guides—to say nothing of quantities of cattle and goats and poultry. In that unfriendly region there was no food to be obtained from the land, and the stores of the refugee party were considerable. . . . But the old fakir was a base traitor, and his plan was a diabolical scheme to utterly destroy the hated whites."

"But there were his own people, too."

"It mattered not to this fanatic that some hundreds of his own people were destroyed," replied Lord Renold. "They were faithful to the whites, and were therefore regarded as deserving of death."

"And what actually happened?"

"No sooner were the refugees within a black and dismal cavern—actually a lofty and deep cave —than the traitor gave word to the lurking rebels. They came in their hundreds, they blocked the tunnel entrance and blasted it with gunpowder. Our short history tells graphically of that dreadful explosion. Many were killed in the blast. Millions of tons of rock fell, for ever blocking the exit. The treacherous fakir and the rebels had committed the white families, as they believed, to a living death."

"By jove, I remember it," said Big Bill, a startled look in his eyes. "I'm not strong on history, but this story you have been telling me is known in our history as the Great Massacre of Yaru. According to our historians, every British soul perished in that gigantic explosion."

"Only a comparative few perished," replied the Lord Renold quietly. "The majority of them lived, they were buried alive. ... But they found that the upheaval of the rocks, whilst undoubtedly sealing the mountain, had opened other rocks at the rear of the cave, revealing unsuspected tunnels and crevasses."

" I get it," said Peter, his eyes shining. " Since there was no way out into the open air, your ancestors explored the crevasses . . . . and found this wonder world."

" Not immediately," said the old man. " Not for many days. The air in the crevasses was found to be pure, and fresh water springs were discovered almost at once. And soon the very rock glowed with its own light—a phenomenon which at first put fear into the hearts of those simple people. Eventually the Lesser Cavern was discovered with a direct way through into the Great Cavern."

He again stretched out a hand.

" At that time, of course, the place was in a state of primeval wildness," he added. " The early struggles were appalling. . . . I cannot tell you of these things now. . . . In course of time our forefathers discovered tunnels and galleries from the Lesser Cavern which ultimately led to the open air, thousands of feet above."

" Where we blew in, what?" asked Reggie brightly.

" In our history it is recorded that there was mad joy when the discovery was first made," said Lord

Renold with a sigh. " One mystery was explained
—the purity of our air. For it was then known
that there was an outlet to the true sky But the
initial joy was short-lived, for exploring parties
made the additional discovery that there was no
way to reach the outer world. A great dip in
the mountains was found, but on every side
were icy slopes which no human being could hope
to climb."

" It hasn't changed," said Bill grimly.

" At intervals attempts were made, of course,"
continued the old man. " Parties went up
equipped with tools to cut steps in the icy slopes.
Some of these parties vanished forever; others
returned defeated by the appalling cold and eternal
blizzards. Thus, young friends, we have never
escaped . . . and we are still at a loss to understand
how you discovered our secret. You have told
us how you entered the cavern, but you have not
told us how you conquered the death wastes of the
frozen mountain."

" Plenty of time for that, sir," said Bill Gresham, with a wry grimace. " As far as I can see,
we're doomed to stay here for the rest of our lives.
It's a certainty that we shall be given up for dead
by the other members of our expedition; and even
if they make an attempt to find us, they'll probably

draw blank or fall into the same trap as we did. It's a pretty bad mess."

Reggie Pickles gave a little chortle.

"Gad! Think of the sensation, though, if we *can* figure a way out," he said with shining eyes. "Why, the conquest of Everest will be nothing compared to it! Think of the whacking great headlines in the London newspapers."

"All you're thinking of, Mustard, is personal glory," growled Big Bill. "What about the people of Lacuna. . . . By the way, why Lacuna?" he added, turning to the High Sheriff. "The underground world had to be called something, I know, but I don't get the significance of 'Lacuna.'"

Lord Renold shrugged.

"One name is as good as another, and 'Lacuna' has a certain smoothness," he replied. "I am afraid our grandfathers were not learned Latin scholars, and our present generation is even more ignorant of that language. However," he added, with a smile, "I think 'Lacuna' is a Latin word meaning a pit, or gap, or void space. Those early councillors of ours no doubt decided that it had a certain aptness."

"Yes, I understand now," said Big Bill. "My own Latin is pretty rotten, too. . . . Gosh, what a triumph it will be if we can get all you people out of this! What a thrill you'll get when you find yourselves in the land of aeroplanes and radio and motor-cars. . . ."

" I wonder!" interrupted Peter Fraser. " The chances are they'll come straight back to this cavern, and think themselves well out of it! I imagine this must be a very peaceful spot. . . ."

He broke off. It did not sound very peaceful at the moment. A sudden tumult had broken out in the town, and it swelled louder and louder. . . . Doors of the banqueting hall were flung open and excited men came bursting in.

The High Sheriff and other dignitaries sprang to their feet, startled by the interruption.

" They come—they come!" went up a cry. " The Jungas are falling upon us from the upper air!"

" The young stranger from the outer world was right!"

" They come to attack us in their thousands!"

Big Bill Gresham caught his breath and clenched his teeth. He made a run for the nearest window, flung it open, and leaped through. Staring up, he beheld an amazing sight.

The upper air of the vast cavern was filled with thousands of slowly dropping " parasols."

Like a swarm of human locusts the enemy was attacking.

Chapter Thirteen
BIG BILL TAKES COMMAND

LORD BILL GRESHAM gave one inward groan. . . .
Just one. Then a fighting light blazed up in his
eyes and he braced himself for immediate action.

Time had been lost—precious, vital time. But
it was no good just standing about and waiting for
the worst to happen. If the High Sheriff had
listened to him in the first place. . . .

Bill ran farther out into the square. Reggie and
Peter were just emerging from the front of the
Town Hall with Lord Renold and many others.
All were staring up into the " sky."

" This is going to be—hot!" Bill told himself
grimly.

His first feeling of blank helplessness was
passing. These people were hopelessly unprepared, the younger members of the community in
particular. Only the older men and women
remembered the despised natives who had been
expelled in disgrace . . . And those natives had
been a mere rabble, incapable of putting up any
organised resistance. The people of Lacuna knew
nothing of the new generation of Jungas.

More than ever Bill was convinced that the

attack had been planned for months ahead. Ordinarily, it would not have happened yet. . . . The savages had been precipitated into hurried action by Bill and his chums. As soon as the Tunnel Men saw their intended victims floating down into the big cavern they decided to act at once, convinced that the comrades would carry the warning. The people of the Inner World were peaceful and unprepared. Only by making a surprise attack could the degenerate Jungas hope to gain a quick and decisive victory.

" Well?" asked Big Bill gruffly. " Do you still think I'm mad?"

The High Sheriff was standing beside him; his face had gone white, and his eyes were full of bewilderment and consternation.

" This is beyond all understanding," he said, aghast. " They fall upon us even as you fell. . . ." He looked at Bill guiltily. " How foolish to ignore your well-meant warning! We might have made some attempt at defence. . . ."

" And we can still make it," snapped Bill.

He felt suddenly savage. Standing here like this, talking, was a criminal waste of time. He spun round, grabbing Peter by the arm. . . . Reggie was with them, too. Another upward glance assured them that the peril was extreme.

The upper air was literally congested with the slowly-dropping Jungas.

"If the air current carries them as we were carried they'll land right bang in the middle of the town," said Bill rapidly. "Listen, you fellows! We three have got to get busy."

"But what the dickens can we do?" protested Peter. "After all, it's not our affair. No reason why we should be dragged. . . ."

"Idiot! It's our affair as much as everybody else's," interrupted Bill. "If these brutes gain the upper hand, we're sunk. Every man jack of us. The people of this place are about as warlike as a basketful of kittens, and you might as well realise that we've got our hands full. The poor saps don't know what war is. . . . Look at 'em."

He flung out a hand, indicating the awe-striken crowds.

"They're not even scared! They don't know what's coming to them. Our pal, the High Sheriff, is the same. Unless *we* take command and organise some kind of resistance it'll be a complete massacre."

"Ye gods, you're right," said Peter, taking a deep breath. "I'll bet the people here don't know of the strange 'fluence the Tunnel Men possess. . . ."

"Of course they don't," agreed Bill. "Didn't

you see how sceptical the councillors were when
I was telling them? There's some natural phenomenon in the other cavern—wherever that may be
—which has got under the hides of the brutes.
Some kind of electrical energy has stored itself
within them. . . . Golly! If it comes to hand-to-
hand fighting, the people will be clubbed like helpless logs. Remember that queer paralysis? It will
grip them as it gripped us. . . . "

He broke off. The picture was ugly. He was
aware, too, that many of the inhabitants of the
big square were regarding him with resentful eyes.
A rumour seemed to be gaining ground that the
comrades had brought this trouble on the peaceful
community.

Bill Gresham soon altered this. He had noted
with satisfaction that the Jungas were drifting
short; they would almost certainly land a full
mile from the town. With so many of them in the
air, the current had lost some of its force.

" That's something in our favour—something
on which the beggars hadn't counted," said Bill
crisply. " It makes a difference. It gives us
time. The brutes won't drop into the town, after
all."

He looked at the helpless, semi-dazed people,
who were just running round in circles or standing in paralysed groups or running into the shops

and houses to find their womenfolk and children.

"Attention, everybody!"

Bill Gresham's voice, loud and authoritative, boomed out like a clarion. Most of the people stopped in their tracks and stared at him. There was something irresistibly commanding in his tone and manner.

"I tried to warn you earlier, but you laughed at me!" continued Bill, quickly seizing his advantage. "If you get yourselves organised, there's still time to give these hairy savages a hot reception. We've got to concentrate on getting the women and children away and building some defences."

As he talked he ran in amongst the crowds. He rallied them, he forced them to pay attention. By the very strength of his personality he awakened a sense of resistance in the peaceful Lacunians. Bill was ever at his best in moments of danger, and he was a born leader. In a very few moments all expressions of hostility had vanished, and men were crowding about him, eager and excited.

"In a few minutes they'll land in the open country beyond the town," shouted Bill, pointing. "Then they'll form up and make a rush. Unless you do something to check them, they'll have the town in their possession inside an hour. They're armed with bludgeons and they mean business.

They'll kill you—they'll kill your women and children—they'll destroy your homes!"

"We must fight!" went up a cry.

"Fight—yes," yelled Bill. "But the women and children and the old people must be got safely away." His eager glance swept round. "Here, you!" he went on, pointing. "And you! And you!"

Several of the younger men stood forward.

"You're strong, sturdy-looking chaps," said Bill briskly. "I want you for leaders. You'll take orders from me, and then organise your own defence forces."

Reggie and Peter, in a lesser degree, were whipping the population into some kind of activity. But it was Big Bill Gresham who assumed full command. His towering strength, his vital power of leadership, commanded obedience. The people of Lacuna not only obeyed him, but were soon obeying him enthusiastically and without resentment.

There was so little time. . . .

Already the enemy forces had floated to the ground. The main body landed, as Bill had expected, more than a mile from the town in open "countryside." A few stragglers were caught by drifting currents, and they dropped separately, but they lost no time in joining their fellows.

Bill had no accurate idea of the enemy's numbers, but he judged that they were between seven and eight hundred strong, and every savage carried a deadly bludgeon. And every savage was a living dynamo, discharging a paralysing current that rendered helpless all who came within arm's length!

A formidable, if primitive, foe!

There was a good deal of confusion in the town. Some panic, too. By Bill's orders women and children and the old men were being evacuated along a good road which led, so Bill understood, to Morganstown, a mile or two away. The Jungas' attack was developing from the other direction.

Bill, bathed in perspiration, rushing here and there, shouting orders until he was hoarse, commanding respect and attention from all, had no time to marvel at the wonder of his achievement. It seemed natural enough that the people should hustle when he told them to hustle.

Hasty barricades were thrown across the one good road which led into the town on the enemy's side. Here and there, at different places, narrow lanes and footpaths existed, but these were of lesser importance, and could be easily held. The Tunnel Men, as Bill had foreseen, were bent upon making a massed frontal attack. They had no strategy. There was evidently no intelligence in their leadership. They were the descendants of savage hill tribesmen, and their environment had only increased that savagery.

" No hand-to-hand fighting!"

Again and again Bill warned the people. Reggie and Peter took up the cry until none but the stone deaf could misunderstand. If they got to hand-grips with the Jungas the town would be lost.

" Ammunition," panted Bill. " We must have ammunition."

Every conceivable kind of missile was gathered behind the barricades. Stones, rocks, hatchets, roofing tiles, and even crockery from the hardware shops and domestic utensils from the houses. Bill's plan was to wait until the enemy was well within range, and then let fly.

" All we need is just one machine-gun," he groaned, happening to come within earshot of Reggie. " That's all, old son—one machine-gun! I wouldn't say ' no ' to a tommy-gun!"

" A few hand grenades wouldn't come amiss, what?" panted Reggie, wiping the sweat from his brow. " Got to be satisfied with these chunks of rock, I suppose. They'll do some damage. . . Hallo! There go the sirens!"

Above the tumult of preparation came a different sound—a wild and unearthly howl. The Jungas, having roughly formed, were rushing to the attack, spreading out as they came.

Bill shouted sharp words of command, and his orders were taken up by the men he had appointed as section leaders. A kind of dread hush fell upon the defences. Out of the corner of his eye Bill caught a glimpse of the High Sheriff himself, valiantly commanding a strong force. . . .

Even Bill Gresham's iron nerves quivered, and he felt his heart thudding. There was something devastatingly fearsome in the charge of the savage Jungas. In the golden glow of the great cavern the brutes looked even more unearthly and hideous than they had looked in the semi-darkness of the upper tunnels.

On they came, shouting and screeching, and brandishing their crude-looking clubs.

" Steady, everybody!" called Bill, his clear voice cutting into the tense hush like a knife. " Don't throw your stones and rocks until I give the order!"

He was mortally afraid that the untrained defenders would waste all their ammunition by precipitate action. That shout of his, indeed, stayed many a hasty hand.

Still the savages came on. . . . And then, while they were still about a hundred yards away from the defences they checked. They checked stupidly. Apparently their eyesight was defective—they were short-sighted—and they had been expecting a clear road into the town. The strong barricades bewildered them.

Bill yelled the word of command.

Instantly the defenders hurled a furious fusillade of rocks and stones. The range was long, but many of the missiles scored direct hits.

The foremost attackers wavered and fell back. But the confusion existed only for a moment. Then the Jungas, instead of making a blind dash for the barricades, did an extraordinary thing. They swung their bludgeons round their heads and sent them whirling through the air.

" Poor fools! " said Peter, staring. " The only weapons they've got, and they waste them by pitching them right over our heads. . . ."

" Waste them? " snapped Bill Gresham. " Look there! Bludgeons, eh? "

He spoke grimly, and with good cause. For the supposed bludgeons, on striking the outlying houses beyond the barricades, gave a curious explosive hiss and burst into violent flame.

Chapter Fourteen

PETER IN PERIL

IT was a dramatic and disturbing surprise.

In less than a minute a dozen great fires were blazing. Many of the houses had thatched roofs, and as the self-lighting fire torches struck, the results were disastrous and spectacular. Flames were soon leaping up in ever-increasing pillars, and the crackling roar of the spreading conflagration struck consternation into the hearts of the startled defenders.

"That's one on us!" said Bill gruffly. "The cunning foxes! Not bludgeons at all, but primitive incendiary bombs! This has been their plan all along—to make one big swoop and destroy the place."

"They're not so savage, after all," said Peter bitterly. "They're employing the methods of the best modern armies! Although they want the town for themselves they set about destroying it as a preliminary! If you ask me, it's just plain crazy."

"Isn't all warfare crazy?" growled Bill. "All aggressive warfare, that is. . . . It's different when you're defending your homes and your lives. . . ." He broke off, frowning. "I wonder why those torches burst into flame?"

173

But it was no time for conjecture. Perhaps the torch heads were made of rock, and fashioned to resemble throwing bludgeons. . . . Bill remembered that the Lesser Cavern contained volcanic fires. . . .

He looked round urgently. Panic was spreading and his presence was needed in a dozen places at once. The whole town was in chaos, and the confusion was increasing.

There was one hopeful circumstance. The Tunnel Men, apparently, were content with their first assault, for having fired many of the buildings, they were retiring. Dozens of houses on the outskirts of Renoldtown were blazing, and the conflagration was spreading with alarming speed.

For there was no way of checking the fire. The inhabitants were not prepared against such a disaster. A dense wall of smoke rose high into the air, blotting out the entire picture.

Lord Gresham thought rapidly.

The town would have to burn. But while the Jungas were pausing, much could be done. Behind the smoke pall Bill quickly organised a general retreat. This decision of his to abandon Renoldtown was masterly and courageous. There was one clear road of retreat—the road by which the women and children had already been evacuated.

The High Sheriff and his councillors, now

thoroughly alive to the peril, staunchly placed themselves by Bill's side and a great deal of panic was quelled. The retreat, at first developing into a rout, became orderly.

" Morganstown is but two miles distant," explained the Lord Renold, his face grave with anxiety. " There is much rock, for the town nestles beneath the cavern side. We may be able to erect effective defences. Thank heaven the people have been got away in safety. But Renoldtown is doomed."

" Can't be helped, sir," replied Bill. " These infernal savages have shot their first bolt, and they can't last long. They relied upon instant success, and they've been robbed of it. There's been no killing."

Before them, along the rough road, crowds were moving fast. Bill had waited until the town had been completely evacuated, and he and the High Sheriff were almost the last to leave. Behind, the smoke pall was more dense than ever; the fire had spread and flames were leaping up in continuous lines.

There was no sign of the Tunnel Men; they were on the other side of the fire, waiting for their grim work to take full effect.

" The poor mongrels haven't the sense to make

a flank attack on us," said Bill. " That's something to be thankful for. . . ."

" Skipper—skipper!"

He turned. Reggie Pickles, panting hard, was running towards him, his face alight with anxiety.

" Peter! Where's Peter?" asked Bill sharply.

" They've got him!"

" What!"

" I want your gun, Bill—it's the only chance," panted Reggie. " It may be too late. . . ."

" Which way?" snapped Big Bill fiercely.

They ran back towards Renoldtown, and were soon off the road, and cutting diagonally towards some outlying burning cottages, ghostly figures in the thick smoke.

" What happened?"

" There was an old woman in one of the cottages," said Reggie breathlessly. " Peter yelled to me, and I went along to rally round. . . . I saw some of the blighting Tunnel Men on the other side of the cottage, and they looked pretty dangerous. Peter and I managed to get the old lady out. . . . The flames were awful. . . . I carried her to one of the last carts that was leaving, and got her aboard, thank goodness."

" And Peter?"

" I thought he was with me," panted Reggie wretchedly. " There was a lot of smoke. . . . I remember, now, that he said something about having another look round, in case there was anybody else. . . ."

Peter, unfortunately, had not seen the Jungas as clearly as Reggie, and he had not realised the danger. And when he had gone through the cottage, and had found it empty, it was too late. Half blinded, half choked, he reeled into the open— only to find himself surrounded by the savages.

He had no earthly chance. In the first five seconds he was helpless. Even in the act of clenching his fists and squaring his shoulders to fight, the dread paralysis seized him. The electrical emanation from the Jungas had him in its grip, and at the first touch he toppled over like a log.

Peter thought it was his last moment. He fully expected to be clubbed to death on the spot. . . . Or worse. Surprisingly, however, he was not immediately killed. The Tunnel Men, uttering wild cries of triumph, whirled him off the ground and carried him away.

But they only carried him a short distance. One of them, apparently in charge of the party, gave an order, and Peter was dropped to the ground. There was a big wooden pole lying nearby; a crooked, twisted pole, long-neglected and lying in coarse grass and bushes. It was the trunk of an old tree, and all the branches had long since been chopped away.

With lashings of creeper, the Jungas proceeded to secure Peter firmly to the very end of the pole, and he was left to imagine what kind of diabolical death they had in store for him. As they crowded about him they kicked at him, spat at him, and expressed their hatred in other ways. Quite clearly they regarded him as a special prize, and were going to give him special treatment.

Soon he was tightly bound and then, with yells of bloodcurdling savagery, the pole was raised from the ground with Peter helpless at the topmost end. The pole was swung round, through the smoke, through the sparks. . . .

Bill and Reggie, plunging through that same smoke cloud, came upon the scene unexpectedly— dramatically. Dashing between two of the burning houses they plunged through a garden and saw in front of them a half-timbered thatched cottage which stood in its own garden. The entire thatch was blazing fiercely.

And close at hand a crowd of howling Jungas were struggling with the long tree trunk, swinging it round at an angle, so that its top would sweep into the very flames of the burning roof. And there was Peter lashed to the end of the pole! In another five seconds. . . .

" The devils!" roared Big Bill furiously.

Crack! Crack! Crack!

Without hesitation, for hesitation would have been fatal, he expended three of his precious bullets. Each one drilled a hole through the head of a Tunnel Man. There was never much wrong with Bill's aim—and nothing at all wrong with it when the situation was critical.

The savages fell dead, and as a result of their sudden collapse the pole wavered and swung back. Peter was still alive—still safe. Big Bill, without a thought of his own danger, ran into the heart of the enemy, yelling at the top of his voice.

At point-blank range he fired again. The sharp explosion struck terror into the Jungas—more particularly as the bullet carried instant death. So near were Bill and Reggie to the enemy that they could feel the strange paralysing effect. If only the brutes had had sense enough to realise their advantage. . . .

It was touch and go. Suddenly, the white-headed savages dropped the pole and fled. Luckily, it was then at such an angle that Peter, at the other end, did not fall far. In a moment his comrades were by his side, slashing at the binding which secured him to the pole.

" Silly ass!" grunted Bill. " Got yourself into a fine mess, didn't you?"

" Sorry," muttered Peter. " That was nice work of yours, Mustard. I saw you get the old woman away . . . The brutes grabbed me before I realised it, and that rummy 'fluence is as strong as ever. I thought my number was up."

They raced back through the deserted town, lucky to get away before the Jungas reorganised and surrounded them. They kept their eyes open for stragglers—for aged or helpless Lacunians who, in the confusion, had been left behind.

But they saw none. In their rear raged fire and destruction; ahead, on the rough road, went the refugees.

" The Tunnel Men may be primitive, and their brain power of C3 quality, but it won't be long before the devils get wind of what's happened," said Bill anxiously. " They haven't had the sense to break through the smoke clouds yet, but we can't expect too much good luck. As soon as they do realise how things stand, they'll be after us like a pack of wolves."

They overtook the rearguard. The High Sheriff was glad to see them. Bill's absence, even for flfteen minutes, had left him anxious.

" This is a terrible calamity, young friends," he said sadly. " For so many years we have been living in peace; and now, with your unexpected arrival, this dreadful catastrophe befalls us."

" I hope you're not blaming us, dash it!" protested Reggie.

" No, no, of course not. . . ."

" This trouble was coming to you, sir, in any case," interrupted Bill. " And although our warning didn't give you much time, at least there has been no serious loss of life."

The old man nodded and looked troubled.

" I blame myself for the disaster which has befallen Renoldtown," he said unhappily. " What crass stupidity to ignore your warnings—to even mock at you! Hours wasted—precious hours, during which my people might have made adequate preparations."

Bill glanced back. Renoldtown was hidden by the vast mountain of smoke which rose in dense masses, and which was already spreading across the cavern roof and diminishing the golden glow. The light of the entire cavern was now pale and unearthly, and full of ominous dread.

" Half-time's up, boys," said Big Bill briskly. " Here they come, full pelt."

Emerging from the smoke pall, like creatures of a nightmare, were hundreds and hundreds of the Jungas. A wild, motley mob, they were running at the double along the road, in grim pursuit of their quarry.

Chapter Fifteen

THE BRIDGE

BILL GRESHAM quickly took stock of his surroundings.

The first glance reassured him. Less than a quarter of a mile ahead arose the crudely constructed wooden towers of a suspension bridge, and across the bridge the refugees were making good progress. The great majority had already passed over.

Some distance away, on a slight rise of the rocky ground, was the smaller settlement of Morganstown, with the sheer wall of the cavern rising in mighty majesty beyond.

"That bridge!" jerked Big Bill, grasping the Lord Renold's arm, and pointing. "Must we cross it to get to Morganstown?"

"Yes."

"There's no other road?"

"None. There is a deep gorge to be crossed, with a swiftly flowing torrent below. One bridge, centrally situated, was sufficient for our needs. . ."

"Good!" interrupted Bill, with satisfaction. "Just that one bridge. . . . That ought to help a lot. We shall have to move fast, though . . .

Mustard! Peter! I want you two chaps! There's a chance we might be able to delay the enemy pretty effectively."

His quick eyes had been taking note of the bridge's construction and an idea had occurred to him. He saw something else, too—something which had put the idea into his head.

" Peter, run forward and stop those four men who look like farm workers," he said crisply.

" You mean the four carrying rakes and things?"

" Yes. Hold them at the farther end of the bridge."

Peter hurried forward without further question. They were all hurrying, in fact. Word had gone forward to the main body of fleeing Lacunians that the respite was over, The savage enemy was hot on their trail.

It was humiliating enough to flee in this way—and from such a lowly foe. Big Bill felt it keenly; his every instinct, his every fibre, urged him to turn and fight. But his sound common sense told him that any such procedure would be sheer folly.

Later on, when the people of Lacuna had had time to efficiently arm themselves, then an attack could be made—and one which would stand a chance of success. At present, unorganised as they were, the only sane policy was to get to the comparative safety of Morganstown as quickly as possible. Its very situation made it much safer as a stronghold than the central city, which had been wide open to attack.

As the townsmen had hastened along the road, workers from the neighbouring fields had joined them, catching the alarm. Some had brought hastily caught up weapons, such as rakes, and spades and scythes and axes.

Bill, calculating distances and time, made some rapid decisions. He had just arrived at the gorge, and he was delighted to see how deep it was—how sheer—how swiftly the torrent raged along its rocky course below. This was a first-class natural defence. The floor of the Great Cavern was split in two by the deep gorge.

The bridge had been built, naturally enough, at the narrowest point of the gorge. On either hand the gorge widened considerably, forming an even more formidable defence line.

" Jove, this looks good," muttered Bill happily.

The last of the refugees were now on the bridge, and the High Sheriff and his immediate attendants were hesitating, looking at Bill for guidance. Everybody, from the highest to the lowest, had accepted Bill's leadership. . . .

" Yes, Lord Renold, if you don't mind," said

Bill briskly. " Go right across. Peter, you'd better go, too. Reggie and I will remain."

None questioned his orders. He glanced back. The enemy was perilously close. Scarcely a hundred yards separated the leaders from the bridge approach.

" Time to shift-ho, what?" suggested Reggie casually.

" Not quite yet," said Lord Bill softly. " Look at 'em, Mustard! We're the ones who make 'em see red. They'd rather have our blood than anybody else's"

" That's what I was afraid of," said Reggie.

" Don't forget how we dished 'em on the upper ledge—how we saved Peter from their murderous clutches. . . ."

" Dash it, old boy, there's no need to remind me," interrupted Reggie, with an uneasy glance at the oncoming Jungas. " The thing that's worrying me at the moment is—what the dickens are we waiting for?"

Bill brandished his fists at the advancing enemy, and a wild howl of execration arose from the savage tribesmen.

" Fine!" shouted Bill. " That's got 'em going! Come on, Mustard!"

They raced across the bridge at top speed. The wooden structure was built on the suspension plan.

There were two high towers, one resting on either bank of the gorge, and the central span was supported by large numbers of ropes which passed over the tops of the towers, and were then secured to roughly made winches some distance beyond. It was a good idea, for when the ropes became slackened by age, causing the span to sag, the winches could be turned and the ropes tightened.

" It's working like a dream," chuckled Bill, as he and Reggie ran side by side. " They're coming helter-skelter, the whole mad mob of 'em."

" You're telling me?" gurgled Reggie, with a glance over his shoulder. " The beggars are gaining on us. . . . Or hadn't you noticed it? I say, this bridge doesn't feel any too sound! Feel how it's shaking?"

" It'll shake more soon," said Big Bill, grinning.

" Eh? I don't see. . . . Well, dash my old school tie! So that's your idea!" ejaculated Reggie admiringly. " What a wily blighter you are, skipper! You stayed behind in order to goad the brutes, and you think that when they mass themselves on the bridge, it'll collapse!"

" That's not exactly the idea, Reggie, but it's near the mark," replied Bill. " The bridge looks pretty strong and it might not oblige us. We'll see what we can do to help."

The bridge's single span was vibrating and

rocking so much that the movements were clearly visible to the eye. The many supporting ropes were creaking and groaning under the strain. Reggie vaguely remembered having read once that an army in crossing a bridge must fall out of step or the rhythm of their marching would destroy the bridge. This crude Lacunian bridge was strong enough for ordinary purposes, but it had never been designed to carry a solid body of raging, prancing, yelling savages.

" Good old Peter," said Bill, his eyes sparkling. " He's standing ready with those four men."

They dashed off the bridge on to the hard rock of the road beyond. By this time the bulk of the refugees had passed out of sight round a craggy hillside, which also hid Morganstown from view. Peter was standing with the stalwart Lacunians and the latter were looking far from easy.

" We run great risk, stranger," said one of them. " The tribesmen will kill if they catch us. . ."

" If," murmured Bill exultantly, " they catch us!"

The bridge was rocking ominously, the span shaking and creaking now that the main body of the Tunnel Men had reached its centre, and beyond. The span was swaying from side to side, and even the wooden towers were groaning as the heavy baulks of timber were strained by the unwonted pressure. The ropes were now twanging drummingly.

'' Good gad!'' said Reggie breathlessly.

He was lost in admiration at Bill Gresham's strategy. Bill had known all along that this very thing was going to happen! The Jungas, swarming like human ants on the bridge, had checked, and panic was growing amongst them. They had felt the grim swaying of the bridge, and were frightened.

It was quite true that Bill Gresham had known what would happen, for his first glance at the bridge had told him that it would behave in exactly this way if suddenly crowded with running human figures. The abrupt checking of the leading Tunnel Men added to the confusion of the others, and the bridge groaned more than ever.

'' Nice work!'' chuckled Bill. '' Now is the time for all good men to come to the aid of the party! Let's see what we can do with these axes!''

He seized one of the implements and set the example. The keen blade whirled above his head and came down.

Thud!

One of the heavy ropes was nearly severed by a single blow. The young Lacunians, and Reggie and Peter, grasped the idea with enthusiasm. They each seized an axe and got busy. And with every mighty blow the ropes were hacked deeper and deeper.

A rope parted with a loud and terrible twang. . . Another rope parted. . . . A third and a fourth. And the fearsome looking Jungas, now recovered from their brief hesitation, were coming on again.

Thud—thud—thud!

Madly, Bill and his companions hacked away. They heard the creaking and groaning increase as rope after rope parted.

And then, with an ear-splitting cataclysm of noise, the thing happened. Sounds like cannon shots rang out as the remaining ropes, unable to withstand the strain, parted in one huge uproar.

And the bridge collapsed like a bundle of great sticks, precipitating the howling Tunnel Men into the raging gorge below.

Chapter Sixteen

THE SIEGE OF
MORGANSTOWN

IT was a staggering sight.

Scores of terrified savages were hurled straight into the torrent, where they were swept helplessly away. The rock sides of the gorge were sheer and there was no possibility of escape—even if the struggling wretches had been able to fight against the force of the torrent.

" Poor devils!" said Big Bill soberly.

" It was their lives or ours," muttered Peter, breathing hard from his exertions, and resting on his axe. " Great work, Bill! You've stopped the brutes, and no mistake!"

The wrecked bridge, most of its debris sagging down to the water's surface, was still groaning and protesting; and the Jungas who had not been thrown into the water were fighting like maniacs to climb back to safety. They were crawling over one another, screaming and crying like animals. It was not a pleasant sight.

" There she goes," said Reggie suddenly.

With a tremendous tumult of splitting timbers the shattered bridge finally collapsed. Unable to withstand the onrush of the torrent, the wreckage parted from the supporting towers and was swept away, carrying scores more of the enemy with it. The remainder of the Jungas were little better than a disorganised mob on the other bank. Many, indeed, were fleeing, terrified by the fate of their fellows.

Bill Gresham took a deep breath.

" Well, that's settled 'em for some hours, I fancy," he said, with satisfaction. " Pity we couldn't annihilate the lot while we were about it. . . . No good looking like that, Mustard. We can't afford to be squeamish. The sooner the beggars are wiped out, the better. More than half the original force is still alive, and they're likely to get reinforcements, too."

He glanced up at the smoke-enshrouded " sky," but there was no sign of further " parachutists." Perhaps there were no more to come. At any rate, it would probably be some hours before a second force could be organised and launched into space.

" We've got time to get really organised, and to fix up some efficient defences," said Bill crisply.

He found the Lacunians looking at him with respect and wonder, and he smiled.

" I suppose you fellows are like the rest of them, eh?" he asked. " You never really believed in these nightmare creatures of the Lesser Cavern? Thought it was just a tale, I suppose?"

" In truth, stranger, we scarce credited the stories we had heard from our fathers," replied one of the men. " Until this day we had never set eyes on any but our own people, for we were born after the Expulsion—as our fathers called it."

" Well, you know now," said Bill, with a touch of grimness. " Thanks for your help. You were pretty quick to get the idea and you worked like Trojans. Well, we'd better be getting along to Morganstown."

" Are all men like you—outside, in the real world?" asked one of the other Lucanians, as they hurried along the road. He spoke tentatively, regarding Bill strangely. " You are so quick—so bold—so nimble."

Bill laughed.

" It's a bold and nimble age—outside," he replied dryly. " I'm afraid you're a bit behind the times in your secluded corner, and in some ways I envy your leisurely mode of life."

" Until this day it has indeed been leisurely, stranger. But this day has changed everything. . . ."

" It'll soon pass," promised Bill. ' If we fight gamely and brainily, we'll have these savages whacked before nightfall. . But you don't have any nightfall, do you? Your native burglars must have a tough time!"

He could see that the young Lacunian was puzzled, and he went on in a more serious strain.

" While we're walking, you might give us some information," he said. " By the way, let's introduce ourselves. Reggie Pickles and Peter Fraser on my left. My name is Bill Gresham."

" Your name is Gresham, stranger?" asked one of the young men, staring. " But that is past belief! *Our* name is Gresham!"

" What, all of you?"

" I am George Gresham, and this is my brother, Robert Gresham," said the young man. " These are my cousins, Kenneth Gresham and Frederick Gresham."

" Well, well, well!" Big Bill grinned. " I'll bet I'm a cousin, too, if you only knew it. About a hundred and fifty times removed. If I look through my family records I shall probably find that a relative of mine was supposedly murdered in the great Massacre of Yaru. Still, that was a long time ago, and we can talk about such things when we have more leisure. What about that information?"

He became brisk and businesslike.

" We shall soon be in Morganstown," he continued, " and I'm glad to see that the place is conveniently near the cavern wall, so it ought to be easy to fortify. How many other towns are there?"

" Renoldtown is our capital—or was," replied George Gresham, with a sad glance at the towering mass of dense smoke in the rear. " Morganstown is the next largest. Llewellyn Morgan is the Sheriff, and a great many of the people are called Morgan. They sometimes call this side of the cavern Little Wales."

" I'm not surprised to hear it," said Bill. " You come from Greshamstown, I suppose?"

The four young Lacunians laughed.

" I am sorry, stranger, but we Greshams have no town named after us," said George. " The Greshams are scattered. Ever since our short history started our families have been farmers; all the farms are owned by Greshams, and they supply the rest of the people with grain and meat and milk and butter."

" And make a good thing out of it, I'll bet," said Reggie, with a chuckle. " Is there any Scottish blood in your family, Bill?"

" We might have known that all the plums would be held by the Greshams," remarked Peter. " A go-getting clan, if you like! Who owns all the banks, by the way? I suppose you people use money?"

The comrades learned that life in the Lost

World went on very much the same as at home, only on a small scale. There were two other towns, and they were on the far side of the cavern— Nortonstown and Sanderstown. They were both small, and really only quiet villages, where the people devoted themselves to the weaving of cloth and the hand manufacture of linen.

At the back of Morganstown, nestling under the cliff, was an iron-smelting works, for here the suitable ore was found in abundance. Morganstown, too, had its timber works and brick-yards and paper mills. Quite an industrial centre.

Over the rest of the miniature landscape farms and cottages were dotted here and there. All the roads and lanes were rough and narrow, for there was but little traffic for them to bear.

Morganstown proved to be a compact little town, with quaint houses, mostly built of a greenish-white rock, which was quarried nearby, and which gave the buildings a very refreshing and bright appearance. All the houses had been erected on a rising plateau, and there was only one real road leading into it, since there was no country beyond the town on the other side

" Looks good," commented Bill approvingly, as they approached " See how sharply the road rises just here? Why, this place is like a fortress. Plenty of rock near at hand, too. Within an hour we'll have half the population at work, and we'll build a six-foot rampart.''

There was intense excitement in the little town; and tremendous congestion, too. Practically the entire population of Renoldtown had sought refuge there, to say nothing of the people from the farms and cottages round about.

'' We've got to get things moving!''

Big Bill, as forceful and assertive as ever, gained an immediate interview with Lord Renold and Llewellyn Morgan, the town's Sheriff. The latter proved to be a tubby, middle-aged, excitable little man who was quite incapable of dealing with the sudden emergency The invasion had left him breathless with consternation.

'' So unexpected!'' he puffed '' So—so disturbing! The catastrophe has taken us completely unawares. . . .''

'' Not completely,'' interrupted the Lord Renold gently. '' My own folly is partly responsible for the disaster. My young friend, here, warned me many hours ago. . . ''

'' Yes, and your young friend!'' broke in the Sheriff of Morganstown excitedly. '' From the Outer World, I understand! His coming, by itself, is the most outstanding event in all our history.'' He looked at Bill's big, brawny frame and forceful face with a kind of awe. '' Such a pity! The nearest thing to a miracle I have ever known, and we are unable to do justice to the occasion, but must perforce give battle to the wretched Jungas!"

"You're dead right, sir," agreed Bill promptly. "And the sooner we make our preparations for battle, the better. Plenty of time for celebrations afterwards."

He was as cool and confident as ever, and easily took complete command. With Llewellyn Morgan himself, and several of the town's prominent officials, he made a quick tour—or as quick as the congested streets would allow.

He suggested plans for organising the defences, and such was the strength of his personality that within half an hour battalions of men were setting off with orderly efficiency to their various duties. Every available inch of house space was given up to the women and children and the older people. Every able-bodied man was pressed into service.

Soon, the place was an absolute hive of industry. Processions of men, with horse-carts, hand-carts, and every conceivable type of conveyance, were carting rock from the nearby quarry; and like magic, under Bill Gresham's supervision, a formidable defence work arose at the top of the rise, just outside the town.

Meanwhile, the smoke pall was lessened, for

Renoldtown was now apparently nothing but a mass of charred ruins. The fire, raging with terrific fury, had burnt itself out quickly.

" Our trouble, of course, is that we don't know the exact strength of the enemy," said Bill, frowning. " We've got to be ready in case the beggars take it into their mad heads to attack again. I'm afraid they're getting reinforcements." He cocked his eye up at the clearing void. " I've noticed a number of those parasols dropping during the last hour or two, and there might be a good deal more."

" Your action, good friend, in destroying the bridge saved Morganstown from a dreadful massacre," said the Lord Renold quietly. " Scarce a man of us was armed, and could have put up but feeble resistance—more particularly as I understand that the tribesmen are possessed of some incredible power which paralyses their victims."

" Yes, we've had more than a taste of it." said Bill grimly. " If it had come to a battle outside the town, with your men unprepared, we shouldn't have stood an earthly. It's a different story now." His eyes glowed as he surveyed the beehive of activity. " With these rock defences, the brutes will have all their work cut out to get near us. We're preparing a few aggressive measures of our own, too."

He was looking out across the " countryside," and waved a hand towards the distant hamlets.

" I don't think we need worry about the people of Nortonstown and Sanderstown," he went on. " The Tunnel Men—you don't mind if I call 'em that, do you?—have little more sense than a herd of gorillas, and they're concentrating on us. It's clearly their object to attack us here, which means they're not attacking anywhere else."

" With those defences we can defy the tribesmen for many days," said Sheriff Morgan comfortably. " Indeed, many weeks.   We have ample food supplies. . . ."

" It's not my idea, sir, to crouch behind defensive ramparts and let the enemy besiege us," said Big Bill, his jaw becoming very square. " Let them make the first attack, yes, but the instant we are ready we'll counter-attack, and wipe the beggars off the map.   Battles are only won by offensive action."

" You speak with great confidence, my dear young friend," said the High Sheriff gravely. " Let us trust that all will transpire as you anticipate. I am certain that our leadership could not be in better hands."

Big Bill grinned—and promptly went off to supervise various matters   To tell the truth, he was thoroughly enjoying himself   This was an adventure after his own heart. He was here, there, and everywhere, lending a helping hand with any difficulty that cropped up. Reggie and Peter, following his example, worked tirelessly.

One of Bill's greatest handicaps was the fact that the men of Lacuna had no knowledge of warfare; they had never handled weapons of war in their lives. They were the rawest of raw recruits. To compensate this, on the other hand, the Jungas were a mere rabble, and Bill was certain that one big counter-attack would demoralise them.

" Their original plan to take these peaceful people by surprise has come unstuck," said Bill. " Whatever else they do now, is doomed to failure."

" You're not losing sight of the fact, old boy, that the Tunnel Men carry their own dynamos?" suggested Reggie casually. " I mean, if these stout chappies come to actual grips with the enemy it'll be all up with them."

" I've thought of that point—and prepared for it," replied Bill Gresham. " It's really quite simple. Our men will carry weapons which will make a nasty mess of the Jungas at long range."

" It's really quite simple?" said Reggie, staring.

" Quite. Lances."

" Eh?"

" Bamboo poles with chunks of sharp rock at

the business end," explained Bill coolly. " I spotted stacks of these poles near the quarries. Not really bamboo, but just as strong. A whole gang is working now making the lances according to my instructions."

" Good gad, you think of everything!"

" It's a good thing there's somebody to think of the obvious ways and means," retorted Bill. " They use these poles ordinarily, I believe, for scaffolding, but that's neither here nor there. My plan is this: after the Tunnel Men have made another attack—and it might come at any minute now—we'll sally out at the head of a strong force. And we can do an awful lot of damage with those lances—and without coming into paralysing contact with the enemy."

Reggie looked dubious.

" Wouldn't be a bad idea to put in a spot of practice, what?" he suggested. " I'm afraid my lancework is pretty rusty. As far as I know, none of us Pickles has used a lance since Agincourt!"

" Well, as a matter of fact," said Bill, ' I'm not too keen on a lance myself, Mustard. You and Peter and I will each grab a nice juicy cudgel and lead the attack."

" Oh, yes?" said Reggie. " Do you think we're charmed or something? What about that beastly 'fluence?"

" My poor fathead, have you forgotten our rubber cold-resisting suits?" asked Bill calmly. " Have you forgotten our oxygen helmets? Why, our very appearance will strike terror into the hearts of the enemy. Don't forget, they haven't seen us with those helmets on. . . ."

" And won't see us," interrupted Reggie sadly. " Aren't *you* forgetting something, old lad? We stripped all that gear in Renoldtown, and Renold-town has gone up in flames."

" What do you take me for?" said Bill scorn-fully. " As soon as I saw the town was doomed I got some of our Lacunian pals to grab the gear and bring it along here. You must think I'm a mug."

" Good old Bill!" said Reggie, relieved. " I didn't say anything, but I was pretty down in the mouth. You see, that oxygen gear is our only earthly chance of ever escaping from this place— and that's remote enough, too."

Big Bill suddenly stiffened.

" Take a look up there," he said, pointing. " There's something that's not so remote. Great Scott! How many of these Tunnel Men are there, anyway? There's five hundred more of them floating down at this minute or I'm a Hottentot's uncle."

Chapter Seventeen

THE BATTLE BEGINS

IT was an amazing sight—and a bit of a shock, too. In the far distance, high up in the great dome of the cavern, hundreds of Jungas were floating down, suspended from their crude parasol-like parachutes.

They resembled a great grey cloud, with the glowing background of the stalactite-studded roof. The last of the smoke from burned-out Renold-town was gone. Bill Gresham's estimate of the number was probably moderate.

" It's queer," he said abruptly. " Some of those things don't look like the parasols, either. They've got some other method of descending." He pointed. " See that bunch over there? They're floating down like a lot of miniature balloons!"

" They can't be all Tunnel *Men,* dash it!" protested Reggie. " I mean, it's not reasonable. They must be Tunnel *Women!*"

" So the whole infernal tribe is planting itself on us," said Bill grimly. " They mean business all right!"

He was undoubtedly right about the whole tribe. But it did not necessarily mean that all the newcomers would engage in the fighting. Perhaps the women—if they were women—were bringing a fresh supply of weapons. This, indeed, seemed the only likely explanation.

" We shan't be long now," said Bill tensely.

He pointed to the other Jungas beyond the ravine. The enemy forces were plainly visible in the now golden light. They were making hasty preparations beyond the wrecked bridge. Almost at once the meaning of the activity became clear. Large numbers of the discarded " parasols " had been brought up, and the Tunnel Men were using these to jump the ravine.

By taking a running leap off the edge of the broken bridge they were able to float across to the other side, the parasols having just sufficient lifting power to carry them. A few fell short, but the great majority got over.

Meanwhile, in the distance, the reinforcements had landed and were hurrying to join the main force. It was difficult to tell what was happening in some parts, for there were some small rocky hills intervening. But there was not the slightest doubt that the Jungas were preparing for an immediate and desperate attack on Morganstown. Thanks to Bill's hectic methods, however, the defences were nearly complete.

A rock wall arose at the top of the rise on which

the town was built.   Behind the wall, which had
many loopholes, the defenders were waiting in
readiness.   All along the wall, against each loop-
hole, were piles of small rocks.   And each rock
was a flint-like weapon.   Men stood at the loopholes with rocks in their hands, ready to deliver
a devastating fusillade at the first onrush

The onrush came. . .

With wild, bestial cries, dense crowds of the
Tunnel Men came surging up the rise towards the
defences.

" Poor, ignorant fools," muttered Bill almost
sadly. " What earthly chance have they got?"

But if the fools were ignorant, they were not
lacking in cunning. Bill Gresham was rash in
wasting any sympathy on them. For suddenly,
just as the defenders were on the point of hurling
their rocks, the attackers came to an abrupt halt
—just out of throwing range.

But not beyond their own throwing range!

It was a shock for Big Bill to see the strong arms
of the Tunnel Men swing back; and the next
moment a hurricane of rocks came hurtling
against the barrier, and over it. Like lightning
the first line of Jungas dropped and the second
line advanced and threw again. There was grim
method in their attack. Cries of consternation and
agony broke out among the Lacunians.

Bill, spinning round, caught his breath. A rock with something attached struck the ground behind the ramparts. There was a strange little puff, and half a dozen men reeled away, their hands clutching at their throats, shrieking.

" Ye gods and little fishes!" ejaculated Bill, aghast. " Poison gas! As I live and breathe, poison gas!"

Poison gas!

It was inconceivable, staggering, fantastic. . . . But, unfortunately, true. The method was crude and only partially effective—but deadly, nevertheless.

Lord Gresham saw that each rock was attached to an inflated bladder. One of the " bombs " which had failed to burst had fallen near Bill, and he picked it up gingerly. The bladder was inflated hard and the heavy stone was tied closely to it—so closely that it indented the bladder. On striking the ground, the bursting of the bladder was almost certain. Or so one would have supposed. Actually, a great many failed to burst.

Bill looked round quickly. This altered things; it altered them drastically. Different tactics were necessary. . . . All along the defence line men had fallen, and some were writhing in agony. Others already lay still.

One of the " bombs " exploded near Bill.

Accompanying the rattle of rock on hard ground came the curious puff as the bladder burst. Bill caught a whiff of vile, noxious fumes as he leaped away. His brain reeled. His throat felt on fire. He backed farther away, and saw that half a dozen Lacunians nearby were down.

There was nothing he could do—nothing much. Holding his breath, so that he inhaled no more of the fumes, he grasped two of the nearest defenders and dragged them clear. His eyes smarted so much that he could scarcely see. By this time the panic had increased, and the defenders all along the rock wall were in retreat.

" Poison gas," muttered Bill between his teeth. " For eighty-five years these people, native and whites alike, have been cut off from the outside world. Yet, when it comes down to brass tacks, their methods of warfare are parallel with our own. So much for the advance of modern science!"

He cast a quick eye over the general scene.

On his right, some distance away, he was relieved to see Reggie Pickles rallying the men under him; farther away, Peter Fraser was yelling like a madman and goading his men on to a counter-attack—but without success. The Lacunians were breaking ranks and retiring. It was a crucial moment.

The Tunnel Men, emboldened by their success,

were making quick rushes, and with each rush they hurled more of the primitive gas bombs, which were now falling well within the defences and popping off continuously. Some distance back more of the savages were massing—in readiness, Bill believed, for a concerted assault.

" If they break through, they'll overrun the town," muttered Bill anxiously. " Once that happens, goodness knows what the end will be!"

Scores of the defenders had fallen. The very nature of their collapse struck terror into the others. Perhaps they knew more than Bill did. . . He rushed up to one of the Lacunian leaders, an elderly tradesman.

" This gas?" he jerked. " Know what it is?"

" Indeed, yes," panted the man. " It is Death."

" But how. . . . I mean, what's the nature of the gas? Volcanic, I suppose?"

" I was a stripling when the Lesser Cavern was blocked, but I well remember what I saw," said the other, his face blanching. " In places, vast cracks in the rock, with boiling fire far below. In other places, strong jets of steam-like vapour hissing with great force from smaller cracks and holes. I was with my uncle, I recall, and he warned me to keep clear, as one breath of the gas meant death."

" I see," nodded Bill grimly. " These devils

have found a way of inflating the bladders. . . .
I'll bet they've been doing it for years, preparing
for the big attack."

" Back, stranger—back!" warned the other
harshly. " The gases are—horrible. Death does
not come at once. He shuddered. " No. Un-
consciousness. . . And then partial recovery,
and hours, days of maddening torture. Do you
wonder that our men are falling back? Many of
them *know*!"

" And the Tunnel Men know they know!"
muttered Big Bill. " Well, something's got to be
done—and done quickly."

He could see that all his strategic plans
would go for nothing unless strong action
was taken. He had imbued the Lacunians with a
temporary fighting spirit, and they had responded
well. But if this panic grew there could be no
chance of ultimate success. Whatever was to be
done had to be done at once.

As cool as ice, Bill's eyes roved bout. He took
in the situation. The bomb attack had expended
its strength; the enemy, he could see, had no
further supplies of ammunition Rashly, they
had hurled all their crude bombs in one grand
assault. Not more than half of the bladders had
burst, and only half of this half had taken effect.

A stupid wastage, proving the incompetence of

the Jungas leaders. With only a little generalship there would have been a very different story. The main enemy force was now getting ready for a mass attack.

" Look out, men!" shouted Big Bill. " They're coming, and we're not going to let them pass!"

The Lacunians, hearing that cry, hesitated. Reggie and Peter took it up—as, indeed, did some of the Lacunian leaders. The Tunnel Men were coming on—a yelling, dancing, gesticulating mob which reminded Bill of a crowd of over-excited Dervishes.

" The lances!" yelled Bill urgently. " Come on, you Greshams—you Morgans—you Nortons! One terrific onslaught and the brutes will scatter. Come on, you Renolds!"

He dashed among the disorganised Lacunians, and was glad to see that Reggie and Peter had not waited to follow his example; they had got busy simultaneously. The Lord Renold himself, the Sheriff of Morganstown, and a few others were adding their own voices.

At first their efforts were useless, but after a number of the townsmen had rallied, others followed their example. Big Bill did not relax his efforts for a second. He kept one eye on the enemy and the other on his men. He could see that it would be touch and go. If the Lacunians made their attack now complete victory was assured. On the other hand, if the Tunnel Men broke through, Morganstown would be lost—and that would mean the wiping out of the entire white settlement.

Magnificently the Lacunians pulled themselves together. Their hearts were stout enough, for they all came of good fighting stock. Never in their lives, however, had they been called upon to engage in battle, and it was only the latent spirit of their ancestors which now came to the surface. Bill did not blame them for their earlier panic. The way in which they now rallied warmed him like fiery wine.

" Fine ! Splendid ! " he shouted encouragingly. " The lances, men ! Get ready ! Stand firm—and when I give the order, attack ! "

He set a splendid example. His original idea was abandoned; there was no time for Reggie and Peter and himself to get into their protective rubber suits and helmets. They would have to take their chance with the rest. They seized the improvised lances, and it was Big Bill who was the first to leap to the top of the defences, his crude weapon high above his head.

" Come on, men of Lacuna ! " he roared. " Charge ! "

He took a flying leap to the ground below, con-

fident that his newly-organised " army " would
follow. And not a second too soon. For at that
very moment the Jungas were starting their own
rush.

A mighty roar went up from the whites. Perhaps it was Bill's example; perhaps their own
fighting spirit was raised to fever pitch by the
sight of the enemy. . . . Whatever the cause, they
charged with a fire and a spirit that was glorious
to see. On all sides they leaped from the defences
and, with their lances ready, dashed at the foe.

The savages checked, surprised.

Clearly, they had expected no such move, and
they were hesitant. That moment of hesitation
was fatal, for before they could recover the Lacunians were upon them.

Chapter Eighteen

VICTORY

It was an appalling clash. In the first onrush scores of the savages went down, spiked by the lances. The poles splintered and cracked, and in many instances the white men and the brown men came to handgrips.

Sudden cries of consternation arose as the Lacunians found themselves stricken—paralysed by the queer electrical emanation from the Jungas.

Fortunately, other lancers were in reserve, and before real harm could befall their comrades they dashed up, and the length of their weapons saved them from close contact with the enemy. More and more of the mop-headed Tunnel Men fell dead and wounded. Big Bill was in the forefront of the fight. His own lance had splintered in the first rush; but, like an eel, he had wriggled back safely out of the way of the paralysing emanation. In a moment he had seized a discarded lance and was again attacking.

" Keep it up, men!" he bellowed.

He had no time during those hectic moments

to see what was happening to his chums; he did not even think of them. He continued to lead the charge, and his stalwart figure, ever advancing, gave strength and confidence to his followers.

" They're wavering!" he roared. ' Come on, men! Just one more rush and they'll be on the run."

He was right. The savages were already wavering. The opposition, and the counter-attack, had taken them completely by surprise.

They had been game enough at first, believing, no doubt, that all the advantage was with them. But as the battle progressed, as the Jungas continued to fall before the deadly lances, they wavered and broke. The realisation that they could not get to close grips with their enemies dismayed them.

Dismay quickly changed to consternation and disorder, and once the rot had started it became a panic-stricken rout.

It spread like a forest fire, and along the whole line of battle the Jungas fell back. Shrieking and uttering unearthly howls in their strange gibberish, they ran. The peace-loving whites halted, now assured of victory.

" They run—they run!"

" We are victorious!"

" The Jungas are beaten!"

Bill Gresham, practically alone in chase of the beaten foe, halted and waved his lance. This was no time to check or hesitate; the rout had to be consolidated.

"After them!" he shouted in a great voice. "Follow me, men of Lacuna—follow me!"

"Absolutely!" yelled Reggie Pickles. "On to victory!"

It was a wise move. As the flushed inhabitants of the Lost World dashed in pursuit of the Tunnel Men, the latter lost most of the few wits which had been spared them. In their panic they took the route by which they had come. And that way lay—disaster.

A moment of thought in that crisis, and the Jungas would have fled to right and to left, spreading out and scattering among the rocky hillocks, and perhaps escaping—or re-forming for another attack. But, like sheep, they ran straight back on their tracks.

Too late the wretches remembered the rock ravine which split the floor of the Great Cavern. The bridge was down, and there was no method of crossing. No time to secure the crude parasols and use them as floats. No hope of spreading out and escaping on the flanks.

They were trapped.

Big Bill, hot on the heels of the hindmost enemy,

prepared to shout a new order. For all his aggressive spirit, he was no cold-blooded killer. He would have given quarter. To spike the Jungas to death while they were helpless was not in his code.

But there was never any question of quarter.

Not for a single second did the Tunnel Men pause or hesitate. Arriving at the brink of the chasm, they hurled themselves straight into space. Such was their panic that they scarcely realised what they were doing. They only knew that the yelling lancers were hot on their heels.

The entire force of Tunnel Men threw themselves into the swiftly-flowing torrent at the bottom of the gorge. As Bill reached the brink and paused, Peter and Reggie came running up from either side. They stood, breathless, watching the luckless creatures being swept away.

"Looks rather like the finish, what?" murmured Reggie, his flushed face grimed with sweat and dirt and blood. "Well, it was pretty hot while it lasted!"

"I think they were all men, weren't they?" asked Bill. "We must have been mistaken about the women—unless they're on the other side of the ravine. A certain number of the brutes never came into the battle at all."

"We shall know later on, when the remnants are rounded up," said Peter. "Gosh! This

river's strong!'' He was staring down into the
gorge and watching the Jungas as they struggled
desperately to keep themselves afloat. '' Reminds
me of the Whirlpool Rapids at Niagara.''

Crowds of the victorious Lacunians were now
on the edge of the gorge, excited with their quick
victory. Bill turned to some of them.

'' Where does this river flow to?'' he asked.
'' Poor devils! I feel sorry for them now. Many
of them are swimming, and I dare say they'll save
their lives. . . .''

'''Tis a matter of doubt, sir,'' said one of the
Lacunians, shaking his head. '' The stream
widens yonder.'' He pointed. '' But it still flows
with great swiftness and the rock sides are
treacherous. The stream flows straight through a
hole in the cavern wall and goes we know not
whither. Those who are carried out of the cavern
will never return.''

Bill nodded.

'' Well, whether they escape or not makes no
difference,'' he said. '' As a fighting force they
are finished. After this reverse they'll never be
able to rally. All you people have got to do now
is to send out ' mopping up ' parties and collect
the stragglers. The war's over.''

He smiled almost grimly. A war lasting only a
few hours! But he knew how different the story

would have been if he and his comrades had not given the warning—if they had not, indeed, taken complete command.

That sudden attack by the " wild men " of the Lesser Cavern would have been a ghastly success, and without question the entire community of Lacunians would have been wiped out to the last man, woman, and child.

" Nice work, Bill," said Reggie, suddenly looking very tired. " Now, perhaps, we can get some real rest, what? I feel that I could sleep for a solid week."

" You're hurt, Mustard . . ."

" A scratch, old boy. Just a splinter of broken lance. . . ." Reggie made a grimace. " I don't think much of those dashed lances, by the way. Most of 'em cracked and splintered at the first touch."

" But they did their work, Reggie—and that was all that mattered," replied Bill. " In any case, there was no other wood available, and you may remember that we were in a bit of a hurry."

Everything seemed strangely quiet after the recent tumult. The last of the Jungas had been swept out of sight. The victory was won. And Big Bill Gresham's thoughts turned upon the plight of his comrades and himself. Were they to be imprisoned in this strange little subterranean colony of England for the rest of their lives?

Little did he dream, in that moment, that the attack of the hairy Jungas was to be the direct means of their own salvation!

Chapter Nineteen

BILL'S BRAINWAVE

THE next few hours embarrassed Bill Gresham immensely. Returning to Morganstown, he was overwhelmed by the congratulations and thanks of the Lord Renold and his people.

As soon as possible he escaped, taking Reggie and Peter with him. Reggie's dream of a long sleep was not realised, for Bill applied himself vigorously to the task of clearing up the general mess and Reggie had to do his bit.

All the wounded and the " gassed " had to be taken care of. Sixteen of the whites were dead; but it was a small price to pay for the victory. The noxious fumes from the bursting bladders had not taken such toll as had been feared; and those of the victims who had inhaled only small quantities of the gas were likely to make a complete recovery.

" It's volcanic vapour, without a doubt," said Big Bill, as he gingerly handled one of the crude " bombs." " Horribly poisonous, too. Either the Tunnel Men failed to fill the bladders properly or the released gas was not concentrated enough to strike death. I mean, the onslaught was only half successful. For half the bladders failed to burst. The only men who died were those who breathed the stuff neat!"

" Does it matter?" asked Peter wearily. " Put that infernal thing down, skipper, for goodness' sake! What a reckless ass you are! It might burst in your hands. . . . What are we going to do with all these unexploded horrors, anyway? There must be hundreds of them lying about, and I'll bet some of them are leaking."

It was a fact that the air in the vicinity of the defence wall was unsavoury. Parties of men were making a collection of the live bombs at Bill's orders. The sooner they were gathered up the better.

" It's funny," said Bill, frowning at the thing in his hand. " This rock is a pretty hefty chunk, and yet it feels extraordinarily light." An idea occurred to him. " By Jove! I wonder. . . ."

He took out his pocket-knife and cautiously cut the binding. Before he could grasp what had happened the gas-filled bladder leaped into the air and soared straight up like a rocket. It was gone so quickly that it was lost to sight within a few seconds.

" Well, I'm hanged! " said Bill, startled.

" You seem surprised, good friend," puffed Llewellyn Morgan, who had observed and who now joined the comrades.

" Surprise is hardly the word, sir," replied Big Bill. " What kind of gas is this poisonous stuff, anyway? Hydrogen is pretty light, but this gas must be three or four times as light. No wonder the stone felt as though it were hollow."

The Sheriff of Morganstown looked reminiscent.

" Forty-five years ago some of our fathers attempted to reach the great outer world," he said. " You see, they discovered the extraordinary lightness of this gas, and in spite of its poisonous qualities they succeeded in securing enough of it to fill a balloon."

" This is mighty interesting," said Bill.

" At that time there was no trouble with the tribesmen, and the Lesser Cavern was open to us all," continued Morgan. " Only through the Lesser Cavern was it possible to reach the tunnels —the upper tunnels which led to the open air— and the great cup in the mountainside which you, yourselves, know of. With great difficulty the balloon was conveyed to the upper air."

" Difficulty!" echoed Reggie, staring. " I should say it was impossible. I mean, some of the tunnels are pretty narrow, and a balloon. . . ."

" The balloon was not inflated, young friend," said the Sheriff gently.

" Oh, I get it! Sorry!"

" I was little more than a lad at the time," continued Llewellyn Morgan, " and I was one of the most enthusiastic workers. It took a number of weeks to prepare. The great balloon, which was made of a specially thin linen, could not be inflated until it was in the open air, owing to the difficulties —as our young friend has suggested—of carrying it through the tunnels."

" How did you manage, then?" asked Bill.

" The empty balloon was carried up, and smaller linen bags, each about a yard in diameter, were filled with the gas. Hundreds of these were carried up, and it was a long and arduous undertaking. Later the gas was transferred to the great balloon."

Morgan sighed rather sadly.

" It was a disastrous enterprise," he went on, shaking his head. ' No fewer than ten men lost their lives, owing to gas leakages. The brave man who ascended in the balloon—his name was Benjamin Gresham, by the way—lost his life, too. I can see the poor fellow now. He ascended rapidly in the little basket, and he and the balloon were soon lost in the whirling mists above."

" The poor chap hadn't an earthly chance," said Bill gravely. " It was plain suicide."

" We did not know that at the time," explained the Sheriff of Morganstown. " Our young men then—myself included—thought of nothing but communicating with the outside world. The venture had been planned for years, and it was hoped that Benjamin Gresham would float beyond the mountain and carry our story to the world."

" You never saw him again?"

" Half an hour after the brave Benjamin had vanished into the mist we saw something rolling down one of the great ice slopes. It was Benjamin. He was dead."

" And the balloon?"

" Benjamin was entangled in the balloon, which was practically deflated. It must have encountered the raging winds above, and was unable to withstand the strain. Benjamin Gresham himself was uninjured. He had simply died of cold."

" Not cold alone," said Big Bill grimly. " At that altitude—away from the pure air of the crater bottom—he rose straight into the rarefied atmosphere of Everest's summit. Naturally, he died. Lack of oxygen killed him, just as surely as the cold. It is humanly impossible for any man to live in such conditions. You didn't know that, of course."

" No further attempt was ever made, for it had proved too costly," said Morgan. " My friend, there is no escape from this little world of ours. We have proved that again and again, and for many

years past our young people have been quite re-
signed to their quiet life here."

Big Bill did not seem to be listening. He walked
a few paces away from the others, his face flushed,
his eyes curiously eager. He was so lost in his
thoughts that he was not aware of a diversion
caused by the arrival of some men who had
thrown ropes across the wrecked bridge, and had
got to the other side of the ravine.

Now they were back with the joyous news that
Renoldtown was not burned out as everybody had
believed. The great fire had destroyed no more
than a third of the city, and the rest of Renoldtown
was undamaged.

There was wild excitement among the Lacunians, and eager plans were discussed for the
making of a temporary bridge, so that the inhabitants of Renoldtown could get back to their homes
and their businesses—so that life in general could
return to normal as soon as possible.

Bill Gresham, still oblivious of what was going
on, hurried to the spot where Reggie and Peter
were still talking to Llewellyn Morgan. The Lord
Renold had joined them, and was, indeed, seeking advice about the remaking of the bridge. They
all stared at Big Bill as his long strides brought
him amongst them, his virile face alight with
excitement.

" Just now, Mr. Morgan, you said that there **is** no escape from this subterranean world," exclaimed Bill tensely. " You're wrong, sir. Another attempt is going to be made—at once!"

" What!" gasped Reggie and Peter in **one** voice.

" My young friend, you are quite mad," said the Lord Renold, almost angrily. " Have you not been told of the terrible dangers? Our experiments over forty years ago proved that no man can live in that dread cold."

" You said the same thing yourself," said Morgan, giving Bill a strange look.

Bill seemed to have gone into a dream again.

" Hundreds of these bladders," he muttered, as though talking to himself.

" Crackers!" said Reggie significantly.

" It must be the strain," murmured Peter, taking Bill by the arm. " Listen, Bill! All you need is a nice long sleep. . . ."

" Hundreds of these bladders," repeated Bill triumphantly. " Heaps handier than a clumsy balloon. No need to bother about the weary, tortuous tunnels from the Lesser Cavern. The bladders will carry me straight up to the hole in the roof, and from there it's easy to get to the open air."

" Bill, for Pete's sake!" gurgled Reggie.

" Don't keep babbling like this! You're scaring me!"

" Listen, boys," said Bill tensely. " Forty-five years ago a man named Gresham tried to get out of this Lost World. To-day another man named Gresham is going to have a shot at it." He grinned with sheer joy. " My dear chaps, it's a cert. The idea came to me half an hour ago, and I've been thinking it all out. . . ."

" You'll go to your death if you attempt any such madness," said Peter angrily. " We won't let you. . . ."

" Rats! There's no comparison between the conditions forty years ago, and the conditions now," interrupted Big Bill. " Supposing my namesake had lived through? He would have descended into a world of desolation—a world of snow and ice and rock. He wouldn't have had a chance in a thousand of making contact with any other human beings. The slopes of Everest are cruel. . . ."

" No need to tell us that," broke in Peter impatiently. " We've had a taste, haven't we?"

" But if I live through, there's the whole of the Gresham-Everest Expedition on the look-out," said Bill serenely. " Now do you get it, Peter? And you, Mustard? Our pals are out there! They're wondering what's happened to us. Old

Bobby Simson is probably flying about this very minute, trying to catch sight of us. . . . Down at the Base Camp they're in a frightful stew, and getting more worried every hour."

" Yes, we see all that," said Peter. " But what good would it be if you dropped into the Base Camp, dead?"

" My poor ass, you're so excited that you can't think clearly," retorted Big Bill. " Have you forgotten our cold-resisting suits? And our oxygen headgear?"

Reggie and Peter stared and gaped.

" The possession of that gear gives us an advantage the people of this Inner World have never had," continued Bill Gresham. " Not if they had tried a thousand times could they have got a man out alive. It was an absolutely hopeless proposition—and that's why they've been lost for eighty-five years."

" Old lad," said Reggie breathlessly, " you've got something!"

" You're telling me?" laughed Bill. " I've got the advantages of modern science—coupled with a crude balloon made out of gas-filled bladders! The bladders will enable me to rise over the mountain and the oxygen gear will keep me alive through the ordeal. Let's get going, boys! The odds are a thousand to one *in favour* of success."

Chapter Twenty

THE GREAT VENTURE

REGGIE PICKLES and Peter Fraser, after scarcely any thought at all, could see the force of their leader's argument. They had in their possession, indeed, the key which would at last unlock the door of this hidden little world.

And they had the Tunnel Men to thank for the chance! It was a curious irony that such should be the case. The very creatures who had sought their destruction were likely to be responsible for their deliverance—and the deliverance of the whole lost community.

Bill was all for making instant preparations. He wanted to have a shot at the experiment immediately, and his enthusiasm was like something alive. But his comrades prevailed upon him to postpone action. They were all dog-tired, Bill particularly, although they had scarcely realised it until now—until the excitement was over.

" There's no further danger, skipper," Peter urged. " There's no violent hurry. And we can't do a thing like this in five minutes, anyhow. We ought to get some rest. In fact, I'm going to see that you *do* get some rest!"

Big Bill laughed and yawned, surprised to find that he was unutterably weary.

" You win, boys," he said resignedly.

So Lord William Everard Cornwallis Gresham slept. He slept for twenty-four solid hours, and Reggie and Peter kept him good company. None of them had quite realised the exhausting nature of the gruelling ordeal through which they had passed—an ordeal which had started long before the fight with the Jungas.

They awakened completely refreshed and ravenously hungry. Bill was glad now that his chums had insisted, for he felt like a million dollars. As he remarked to Reggie, if there had been a bus handy he would have pushed it over.

The Lacunians had not been idle. After all, their own ordeal had been confined to a few hectic hours, and life very quickly resumed its normal leisure. The few scattered Jungas had been rounded up and conveyed to a remote corner of the Great Cavern, where they could be easily kept under vigilance. The bridge had been patched up, and the trek back to Renoldtown was practically completed. When Bill heard these details he could not help grinning.

" A fat lot of faith these people have got in my scheme!" he said. " All this activity shows that they're calmly returning to their usual ways, fully expecting that nothing will come of my venture. But we'll show 'em! At least, I shall. You two will stay here. . . ."

" We were going to talk to you about that, skipper," said Peter, almost aggressively. " The people have been gathering up the gas-filled bladders, and there are a lot more than you need. Plenty for the three of us, in fact. . . ."

" Fine!"

" All we've got to do. . . ."

" But I'm going alone, all the same," continued Bill calmly.

" Now, look here, skipper. . . ."

" I'm going alone," insisted Bill. " You two will stay here. I thought it all out before I went to sleep."

" But that's crazy!"

" Listen, Peter! It *would* be crazy for all three of us to make the attempt," said Bill soberly. " I'll go first, and I'll go alone. . . ."

" What about drawing lots?" suggested Reggie brightly. " Or tossing? Or choosing straws?"

" Nothing doing, old son! As leader of the expedition, I'm going to insist on my rights, and if you argue until you are blue in the face it'll make no difference." Bill was rock firm. " If you hear nothing after, say, a month, you can be pretty certain I've failed. Then you can do your tossing or choosing straws as to who tries next. Not that it will be necessary. Even if I'm dead. . . ."

" Oh, I say!" protested Reggie.

" Even if I'm dead," insisted Bill, " they might find my body, and I'll carry a written message on me, fully explaining the situation."

" They ' might ' find your body," grumbled Peter. " Supposing they don't? What about us? How can we be rescued? Perhaps I'm talking selfishly, and if so I can't help it. It's not so bad for the Lacunians—they've never known anything else. But we want to get out—we want to share in the sensation that our story will cause. . . ."

" If I get through the rest will be easy," interrupted Big Bill. " Just a matter of time. Knowing what we have to face, a party of us will make the climb; we'll bring ropes and lower ourselves into the great crater. Meanwhile, the wireless will be busy, and the world will be electrified by the news, and an expedition fifty times as big as our little show will be organised."

" By jove, yes," said Peter, his eyes shining. " As soon as the news gets out, there'll be a whole army corps on the job, complete with stores, supplies, aeroplanes and everything! It'll be a Government job—not merely a privately financed show!"

" Exactly," agreed Bill. " And when I get the

British Army and the R.A.F. boys on the job. . . . Well, there's no more to be said. The rescue of the whole Lacunian people will follow as a matter of course. So let's go and have a look at those death bladders. . . . Death bladders, eh? That's rather ironical, for to us they mean life!"

After careful experiment the exact lifting power of the noxious gas was calculated. Many dozens of the bladders were tied together, attached to long strings, with a little carrying cradle beneath.

The remainder of the bladders were carefully stored away—for possible future use. A grim thought, this. . . . Altogether the preparations occupied two full days, but at last everything was ready.

Big Bill, completely attired in his cold-resisting suit, with his oxygen helmet slung handily over his shoulder, went to a spot beyond Renoldtown, in the very centre of the Lost World. Crowds of enthusiastic Lacunians had charge of the " balloon ". Immense throngs of other people, including women and children, were there to give Bill a great send-off. In their eyes he was a kind of magician, and while hating to see him go, they felt that all their hopes for the future were in his keeping.

There was no nonsense about the matter-of-fact Bill. A quick handshake with his comrades, and with the leading men of Lacuna, and he gave the signal. A wave of his hand, and he rose sluggishly into the warm air. The " lift " had been gauged exactly, and the ascent was perfect.

" So long, you fellows," sang out Bill, from a hundred feet. " I'll be seeing you!"

Reggie and Peter found it difficult to respond to that hail, owing to the choky feeling in their throats. From the crowds came a mighty roar of God-speed. High above Bill was the " hole in the roof " of the Lost World. If the drifting air currents did not carry him astray, he would float straight up towards that outlet. He carried with him a long pole, for there was a danger that the bladders would strike against the roof stalactites and burst themselves.

As a matter of fact, it was a near thing.

Bill reached the roof seventy or eighty feet away from the exit-hole, and the long pole saved his life. With its aid he managed to edge himself along until, at length, the balloons rose easily through the opening. A ticklish business, and fraught with much peril—but successful.

There was one very important point which Bill had thought of. The lifting power of his balloons would have to be very much greater if he was to have any chance of rising through the rarefied Everest atmosphere, and battling through the eternal hurricanes. He had therefore attached heavy weights to himself, and by the simple act of discarding these now, the bladders were doubly effective.

The odds were that he would shoot up like a rocket, and it was likely enough that many of the bladders would burst. If they didn't burst, Bill himself could burst them, in order to regulate his descent. The gas would be harmless, since he would be wearing his oxygen gear.

It was a long, slow business, conveying the precious bladders in small groups through the tunnels to the upper air. Bill never knew how many hours he spent on this task. He was keyed up to a high pitch of excitement and enthusiasm. But at last he was ready. . . .

He stood there, alone, in the basin of the immense extinct crater, with its sloping rock sides, with the upper reaches mere sheets of glacial ice. He looked into the eternal mists far above—and saluted.

" Okay, Old Everest!" he shouted. " Here I come!"

He fixed his headgear, made the final adjustments, and rolled the heavy rocks away from the anchor rope—the rocks which had been keeping the " balloon " to the ground. Like a rocket he soared straight upwards into the swirling mists, and he experienced a sensation so devastating that he had an idea he had left his stomach behind.

Up and up! Then the mists claimed him, and he was gone.

To his dying day, Big Bill Gresham was destined to remember that appalling ordeal. He suffered no discomfort in breathing, for his oxygen supply was steady and regular. He suffered nothing from the cold.

But . . .

No sooner had he ascended to the region of the everlasting blizzards, caused by the impact of warm air on cold, than he thought his last moment had come. Like a shuttlecock he was tossed this way and that. At first, blinding mist surrounded him; then swirling masses of snow.

One second he was shooting straight up into the heavens, and the next he was dropping like a stone, completely at the mercy of the terrible wind currents. His brain was numbed by the buffeting he got; and, indeed, there was a period that was a complete blank.

Certain death, he felt, was inevitable. He could never come out of this alive. Owing to the terrific strain, the bladders were bursting and others were tearing away. Whirling round like a top, at one moment upside down, and the next moment right way up, he was suddenly aware of the fact that he had been shot out into clear air.

He blinked in the sunshine. It was some moments before he could gather his wits—before he could see. He knew that he was dropping, and dropping fairly swiftly. His first glance showed him the bunch of bladders. . . . Less than half their original number, and insufficient to sustain his weight.

But he saw something else—a sunlit vista of icy glaciers and mountain slopes.

He was through!

He had been cast out from that maelstrom of hurricanes. And the next thing his gaze encountered was—a plane! Less than a mile away, it was flying sedately. Frantically he waved. . . . An unnecessary gesture. For at that moment the plane dipped and came zooming round in a vertical turn. The pilot—probably Bobby Simson himself—had seen him! Good old Bobby! Scouting round for some sight of the lost climbers. . . .

Big Bill laughed. Bobby's eyes were probably bubbling at the unexpectedness of the sight he had seen. The plane came roaring nearer; and by this time Bill was descending into a great snowfield, far down the mountainside. A soft place on which to land—within easy reach of friends—and safety!

Guided by the plane, a party of climbers set out

immediately, but many hours were sped before Bill was reached. . . . And then his rescuers were firmly convinced that the poor fellow had gone completely out of his mind. The story he told was too fantastically impossible to have any relation to the truth. Reggie Pickles and Peter Fraser were dead, of course; they were lying stark in the snow. . . .

However, there were the gas-filled bladders to explain away, and the carefully prepared message, signed by all three comrades and the High Sheriff of Lacuna, which Bill carried. . . These things could not be the product of Bill's distorted imagi-nation. They were startlingly real.

In the end, of course, he convinced the other members of his expedition that the extraordinary adventures had really happened; and then the Gresham-Everest Expedition went wild. Then the radio crackled forth the staggering story.

Never had the world known such a sensation as that which burst upon it. People in every country flatly refused to believe it, saying that it was just a sensational stunt. Not until Bill Gresham reached England—by plane to India, and then by swift air liner—was he able to get things moving. But after that they moved fast.

His story was water-tight, and the proofs he brought were completely convincing. The British

Government organised the mightiest Everest Expedition ever. A vast armada of air liners, supported by land forces. That climb to Everest's summit was sensational in every way, for it was not accomplished by a few daring spirits, but by a force numbering many hundreds.

Supplies were carried—ropes, miniature balloons, rubber suits and oxygen equipment for all the inhabitants of Lacuna. And thus every living soul of the People of the Lost World was rescued—and brought to the Greater World they had heard about and dreamed of. For them it was akin to a miracle; for Reggie and Peter it was just another exciting adventure, and their reunion with Big Bill was deliriously joyful.

The remnants of the Junga tribe were left in the Great Cavern. Such creatures could not be brought into the ordinary world—and, in any case, they had now achieved their ambition. They had the Cavern to themselves, including the towns and farms and all the livestock. Better that they should be left just where they were.

Bill Gresham and his two comrades were the heroes of the hour, for they had saved a long-lost British community from oblivion.

" So long, grim old Everest!" said Bill, taking his last look at the mighty mountain. " We wrested a queer secret out of you, but you're still

Everest the Unbeaten! It's a pity, boys, that we never really got to the top!"

Reggie and Peter grinned. There was a speculative note in their leader's voice, and a determined twinkle in his eye. . . . But the odds were that some other exciting part of the world would take possession of Big Bill's imagination, and lure him away to fresh adventures.

THE END